REIGN

A Skulls Renegade Novel

Book #1

COMING SOON FROM
ELIZABETH KNOX

Redemption
(Skulls Renegade #2)

Tough as Steele

REIGN

A Skulls Renegade Novel

Book #1

Elizabeth Knox

REIGN

Cover Design By CT Cover Creations
Editing & Formatting By Cordially Chris Author Services,
www.cordiallychris.com

ACKNOWLEDGEMENTS

BECCA – Thank you for being the first to read this, I was shocked when you fell in love with the MC romance world, but don't worry, I'll have plenty more for you soon.

KAIT – I can't express how your honesty helps me make these books bigger and better than I could've ever imagined. Thank you for listening to my crazy plot ideas, time after time.

MY LOVELY BETA READERS – You are so amazing! Each one of you has stepped up to the plate and have given me such valuable feedback.

MY AMAZING COVER DESIGNER, CLARISE TAN – You see my vision and transform it into something real. You're so talented, and I'm so lucky to have you working with me.

MY EDITORS, NORA BENEDETTO & CHRISTINE BORTNER – Thank you so, so much for working with me!

MY READERS – Enjoy the ride guys because it's about to be a crazy one. I hope all of you fall in love with Elena and Reed's story like I did when I was writing it.

DEDICATED TO CHRISTINE

You've dealt with my every question and nagging concern through the development of REIGN and CORRUPTED LOVE.

Thanks for being the best surrogate mom, writing coach and all around amazeballs person and supporting me in my big dreams of becoming an author.

I don't know how I would've gotten this far without you!

Love ya!

WARNING

This content contains material that may be viewed as offensive to some readers, including graphic language, dangerous and sexual situations.

PLAYLIST

I Don't Wanna Live Forever |

Taylor Swift & Zayn

Fighter |

Christina Aguilera

Bad Girlfriend |

Theory of a Deadman

Confident |

Demi Lovato

Bad Things |

Machine Gun Kelly & Camilla Cabello

Criminal |

Britney Spears

Shameless |

Sofia Karlberg

R.I.P. |

Rita Ora & Tinie Tempah

Ain't My Fault |

Zara Larsson

PROLOGUE

Elena

It was absolutely freezing in Cincinnati that day as I headed out in my black trench coat. I'd say it had never been colder, but I just happened to be in a state of undress that allowed the cold to chill me to the bone in a way it usually wouldn't.

I was going to surprise Rich, my fiancée, at the office. He had just got promoted to being a full partner at the law firm, and things had been a little tense with us. Hell, things had been shitty to be totally honest.

We hadn't had sex in months. He had been working late a lot, and yeah, I knew it was because he was working so hard to make partner, but I am a bit of a selfish person when it comes to romance. I just wanted to get back to the way we were. We were getting married in three short months, and I just felt it was time to get back on track. We had admittedly both been too busy with work; me with the FBI, and him trying to make partner.

I was sure it was really a great moment to make up for lost time.

I had the whole thing planned. I was going to bring him coffee in just a black trench coat.

Literally. That coat was the only thing covering my birthday suit.

I strolled into Starbucks right around the corner from his office and ordered us both a coffee. A peppermint mocha for me and a café latte for Rich. The smell of peppermint made me so excited for Christmas next week, Rich and I were getting two uninterrupted days together, which rarely ever happens.

I walked into the law firm, and Shirley, the receptionist, was the first to greet me. "Miss. Elena, what a surprise!" I had come to love the older woman who manned the desk; she was the epitome of grandma with the curly white hair, adorable glasses, and she even has that overly concerned voice.

"Hey Shir," I walked around the desk and gave her a hug, "How are you?"

"Oh, I'm just great. I can't wait to see the grandkids next week!"

"I can only imagine, I'm sure you're going to spoil those kids rotten," I told her. Shirley giggled at my comment. "Anyways, I was going to pop by to see Rich for a moment and give him some coffee. Is he in his office?"

"Let me check." Shirley tapped away on her computer, the sound of clicking entrapped me. I should've called first and made sure he was available. How stupid of me. He was going to be busy since he was a partner. Dumb Elena, dumb.

"Oh yes, he is available. He should be in his office. It was nice to see you dear, and if I don't see you, I wish you a very Merry Christmas."

"Merry Christmas, Shir." I smiled at her, walking back the long hallway where Rich's new office was. The law firm he worked at was one of the biggest in Cincinnati, and he'd been fighting since he was a first-year associate to get that coveted promotion. I was glad he finally got what he deserved. Rich was an extremely hard worker, and I couldn't be prouder of him.

I came up to Rich's office, opened the door and walked in.

"Oh yeah…baby just like that!" was the first thing she heard upon entering his office. Rich was slamming his dick into some blonde woman over his desk, and she moaned as he pounded into her.

I was frozen. What was I supposed to do?

Am I the woman who runs out of his office crying? Or am I the woman who tells him to go fuck himself?

I was watching him fuck this girl, thinking about the five years that I invested into our relationship. Was this the first time? It probably wasn't.

I couldn't believe I had been that naïve.

"Dick." The moment my pissed off name for him came through the room, he stopped, staring right into my eyes. The shock written all over his face almost made up for the thick betrayal I was just handed. "Oh – Shit El, it's not what it looks like."

"Well, it looks like you have your dick shoved up someone who isn't your fiancée. So, tell me, how is that not what I see right now?" I crossed my arms, tightening my trench coat. He didn't deserve that show anymore. My plan was for him to be fucking me over his desk. That wasn't going to happen now.

He slid out of the woman, putting his trousers back on. She scurried off into his attached bathroom, escaping from the screaming match she thought we were about to have.

"I cannot believe you," I ground out. "You're such a piece of shit; you know that? I didn't complain about you working late hours; I supported it because I knew how much you wanted this."

I moved my hands around the room. "I knew how much you wanted to be a partner. Now, all I can think is that you were fucking other women this whole damn time." I took off my engagement ring, throwing it at him. "You may be a partner, Dick, but you sure as hell don't have one."

I march out of his office, leaving him gaping at me. Maybe he thought I'd forgive him; I wouldn't. I can forgive a lot of things, but I will not and never will forgive a cheater. Once you destroy trust, you don't get it back.

There's only one thing I could do now. I didn't want to go back to our condo. I knew I had to go and get my things, but after that, I would do the one thing that would help me.

I was going to bury myself in work.

CHAPTER 1

Elena

"Are you sure you want to do this? You haven't been in the field in six years. I'm not just your handler; I'm your best friend. I'm worried about you." Kristie was my best friend; we had met at Quantico and went through the same training program. It was a pleasant surprise when we both were assigned to the Cincinnati field office. Kristie loved being a handler, but I didn't. I took the job when things with Rich got serious because he expressed how worried he was for me if I was on the field. So, I made that sacrifice, for our relationship; I stopped doing what I loved and became a desk jockey.

I loved being in the field, the rush, the thrill of it. The adrenaline pumping through my veins gave me the best feeling in the world. I felt invincible, and I was. I was until I got shot in the shoulder. The docs said I would never be able to return to field duty, but I never was one who liked to be told what was or wasn't going to happen. So, what did I do? I proved all the docs wrong and came back stronger than ever.

"Kristie, I need this. I gave up so much of myself for Rich, and then that bastard lied and cheated, throwing everything I did for him in the trash. I need to go back to being Elena, the kick ass field agent. I need to take down some bad guys. I need to feel like myself again." It was the absolute truth. I was beginning to realize that over the past five years I had felt like a robot. Like I had only been here to please Rich, not to do anything for myself, but everything for him.

"I can't condone that your shitty love life is the reason for going back in the field. But as your handler, I know what type of asset you are to the bureau."

Because I'm kick ass, she doesn't have to say it, but we both know it.

I leaned back, slightly sinking into her couch, pulling her fluffy blanket closer to my chest. "So, what's my assignment?" I grinned like a kid on

Christmas morning. Ironically, it was Christmas Eve, but still. I was experiencing the same effect.

Kristie handed me a folder, and I opened it, skimming over the documentation and photographs. "Skulls Renegade MC, huh?" I flipped through the rest of the paperwork, looking at the photographs of the main members, plus some history on each of them. There wasn't much intel, just birthdates, socials, where they were from. "They've kept quiet," I muttered. Kristie took a sip of her bottle of wine.

"Yes, they have. But not quiet enough. We have an informant saying they're doing some major drug trading and they're in a prostitution ring. You're going in to find out what's really going on. Gather enough intel, issue warrants and get out. These are brutal criminals, El. Taking them down would blow up both of our careers."

Like I needed to know what kind of men are in the MC lifestyle? I didn't need a reminder. "I've got it covered." Kristie handed me another folder.

"This is your cover story."

I opened it up, looking at the profile they'd created for me. Kristie knew me well enough to know I wouldn't use it, so what was the point in even showing me? On every assignment I'd ever been on, I'd been given a profile to study: dates, times, life events, other crap. I had to make my cover real. I understand the important of that, of course, but it had always been easier for me to alter my own profile. That way I didn't slip up. The bureau never did like the way I operate, but they didn't say a damn thing anymore because I always got the job done.

Kristie handed me a burner phone. "You'd better call me every Monday at ten in the morning with updates. I mean it."

I smiled at her. "You got it, boss."

***

I left the next morning; Christmas Day. There wasn't a point in staying around now that there was nothing tying me down. Plus, I needed an outlet for my anger and pain, and quick. This was going to be my redemption job. My way to being the Elena I could recognize when I looked in the mirror.

I packed two duffel bags full of necessities; clothes, shampoo, and makeup. I hopped in my 2017 Ford Mustang and hit the road.

Destination: Tennessee

It took me six hours to get there; the MC was located right in the mountains in the small town of Gainesville. It was truly a small town. There's a bank, a couple restaurants, a grocery store, law office, daycare, school, and not much else.

I found a half-way decent room at the only motel in town. From the looks of it, it probably had roaches. The sooner I could get into the club, the better. I wouldn't be getting an ounce of sleep in that shit hole.

I took a quick shower, cringing because the white tile was yellow. They had a 'cleaning service,' but I doubted it had been properly cleaned in years.

I dried my hair, applied some makeup, and dumped all my clothes out on the bed. My plan? Go to the biker bar, get a few drinks, and make my presence known. My tactic? Easy.

I was going to dress like an Ol' Lady, not like some stupid little skank who comes to the bar just to suck their cocks. I learned from my mother how to dress the part. Ol' Ladies aren't there to service the men. I sure as hell would not be there to do that either. I was going to be walking in like I owned the place because I did.

These bikers were going bow on their knees when I walked in because I bet you no bitch had ever dressed as I was about to.

I grabbed a pair of black leather leggings and black heels; the heel so thin that stepping the wrong way could crack it. I found a thin, jersey type tank top and paired it with my emerald green leather jacket. I pulled my hair out over my jacket, the loose curls bouncing over my breasts. I went into the bathroom, applied a little more eyeliner and touched up my neutral matte lipstick. I slid on my metallic aviators and went for the front door.

I was good to go.

CHAPTER 2

Reed

"Where the hell did that fine piece come from?" Enzo grumbled, staring right into the doorway of Bubba's.

"She's gotta be new," Max added.

She was. I'd never seen her in Gainesville, and I know every single person. It was my job to. If I'd seen this hot siren come into my town before, I'd fucking know.

She was no club whore; that was a fact. She was dressed in head to toe leather, her perky breasts visible from the low scoop of her shirt, and that fire red hair of hers was intoxicating. My cock was already twitching.

"No one touches her," I growled at the men around me, making them all nod in accordance. I was the Prez, and whatever the fuck I say, goes.

"Why you gotta always call dibs on the hot ones?" Seamus asked, and I shot him a death glare. He just laughed it off. He may have been the strongest member of my club, but he was also the stupidest.

I turned back to the woman who was blowing my mind and watched her for another moment longer. The way this woman walked, she acted like she owned the place, and dammit, she could. She was a siren for sure; a woman to be reckoned with. And she just walked right past me, smirking slightly.

I looked on her leathers for patches, but there weren't any. That was good; it meant she wasn't an Ol' Lady. She wasn't committed to a club, or a man. At least not yet.

That was about to change, and I was going to make damn sure of the fact.

She may not have known it yet, but she was mine.

****

Elena

Bubba's was the only bar in Gainesville. I thought the biker bar would be harder to find, but it wasn't. They really made it easy for me. I slid out of my Mustang and walked into the bar. Before I even went through the doors, I noticed eyes on me; my plan was working.

I pulled my aviators off walking into the bar, sliding them into the small black leather fringe purse I brought with me, completing my biker chick look.

I glanced around the bar, looking for that empty barstool I wanted. Instead, I saw my target.

Reed Michaels, President of the Skulls Renegade MC.

The pictures didn't do him justice. They had to be old because he wasn't the muscular man I was looking at now. His tribal tattoos came out from his fitted tee. His stare was on me, as were the rest of the men's.

I walked straight past him, getting a whiff of sandalwood and old tobacco. I'm not a fan of the smell of cigarettes, but that wasn't it. It reminded me of chewing tobacco. Now that always smelled good despite the bad habit that came with it.

"What can I getcha, lady?" A tall woman with jet black hair asked me. She struck me as a lifer with a get up as close to mine as I saw in the place, though it was a little skimpy for my tastes. It was probably part of the job, though.

"Jack n' Coke, please." I handed her a twenty, urging her to keep the change.

She walked away, coming back a few minutes later with my drink. I took a sip, and it was pure perfection. "You look like a woman on a mission," the women commented. "I'm Daisy." She extended her hand. and I shook it.

"I'm Elena"

"So, what mission are we on tonight Elena?" She winked at me, surveying the bar.

"I'm looking for some good cock." Daisy laughed at me, but I wasn't lying. I was looking for some sex. who said I couldn't be on assignment and enjoy some mind-blowing sex too?

"There's plenty of that around here, sista," she told me with a grin. Was I irresponsible? Probably, but I hadn't had sex in two months. Two months of my hormones being jumbled up and being completely unsatisfied.

Your own hand can only do so much.

"I don't think you're getting any cock, except Reed's, though," she commented. Reed. My target. I supposed the prez probably did get dibs on new women unless he already had an Ol' Lady, but Reed was young for a prez.

Being with him would be crossing the line a little bit, but….

"Who's Reed?" I asked knowing all too well who Reed Michaels was. Daisy pointed to the end of the bar where the man's eyes were locked to my body. Maybe it was the alcohol, but he looked even hotter now. His black hair was slicked back like an old-school greaser. A few days of not shaving amped up his sex appeal for me. His bulging muscles coming out of that tee, and those tattoos were a major turn on in my book. I felt like I was staring into the eyes of a cover model for Inked.

"Ah" I chuckle, taking another sip of my drink.

"What's your story? I ain't ever seen you around here," Daisy questioned politely.

"I'm new to town, I just came in today," I admitted, wanting to keep things as authentic as possible. Though, Kristie would probably choke on her morning coffee if she knew I was being so honest and using my own name.

"You stayin'?" I like her boldness to fish for information. In another life, we probably would've been the best of friends.

"Yeah, I think so. I need a change of scenery. I walked in on my fiancé fucking his secretary. Adios!" I waved my hand up dramatically, taking another sip of my drink. Daisy's face dropped open. Was that a little too much honesty? At least scorned woman was a part I could play without trying.

"Girl, I know we just met but what're we gonna do? Light some shit up? Poison his girl?" I laughed loudly at the poison comment.

"I handled it," I added with a wink for effect.

"I bet ya did sista; I bet ya did!" Daisy stayed quiet for a moment, "Now, let's get ya some sex!" She said a little too loudly; a few heads turned into my direction. I had to laugh it off because I wouldn't be mortified by her outburst. I liked this girl; I really liked her.

Daisy and I chatted for a while; I found out as much about her as I could. It wasn't much. She was from Baltimore but moved out to Tennessee when she turned eighteen. Daisy had been working at the bar for four years now. "What about you, where you from?"

"I'm from Texas, but I moved away when I was really young."

"Ya look like a Texas girl; everything about cha screams bad ass chick. What's the saying 'Don't mess with Texas'?"

"You got it!" I wasn't lying; I am from Texas. Austin specifically, but that was in my past. I left Austin, TX behind when I was seventeen and never looked back. I don't think I ever will.

"Babycakes!" A woman shouted from behind us, another one was next to her, sliding onto the two barstools next to me. Daisy greeted both women.

"That's Jenna," Daisy pointed to the brunette, "That's Michelle," Daisy pointed to the blonde.

"And this is Elena; she's new to town. She moved down here after she found her fiancé cheating on her with his secretary." Daisy was quick to share the savory piece of gossip. There was nothing better for women to bond over than an asshole cheater.

"Is this an episode of Days of Our Lives?" Michelle said, her mouth hitting the floor.

"Nope, just my life" I laughed.

"We're on a mission to get Elena laid. I think Reed's gonna fulfill her needs."

Michelle and Jenna both looked past me, to the end of the bar where Reed was sitting. "Mhm!" They both mumbled simultaneously, giggling into their chests.

"What's his story?" I asked the ladies while Daisy refilled my drink. "Reed is…"

"mysterious."

"unpredictable."

"sexy as hell."

"Well damn, not a lot to go on," I joke, the girls just nod and smile. I'm surprised with the turnout of people that were there on Christmas. It was in the late evening, so maybe they'd all had their own

Christmases and then headed to the bar. I wouldn't know much about that; it was usually Rich and me.

Now it was just me.

"Get some music on! I'm dying!" Jenna dramatically clenched her heart. "Tell me it's not Christmas Carols, though,"

"Fuck no!" Daisy laughed, she pulled a remote out of a drawer, turning on the music system. "I feel inspired by your situation."

A second later, Christina Aguilera's Fighter came over the speakers. Daisy lined up six shots of tequila in front of us, and I shot back two, and the others disappeared. "Let's get dancin' ladies!"

Jenna dragged me onto the dancefloor; Daisy and Michelle were right behind us.

I swayed my hips to the beat, letting loose a little. Nothing could happen to me dancing in a biker bar, at least, nothing I didn't want to happen. Jenna ground her ass against me. I returned the favor, my hands going over my head, grinding my ass to the beat. "This is about cha girl!" Daisy yelled over the music. I cocked my head back and laughed.

Hanging around these ladies, I felt like I had known them for years. I was just comfortable with them. They were going to be me in, I just knew it.

Theory of a Deadman's Bad Girlfriend came on next. We stayed out on the dance floor grinding up against each other. One by one the girls were met with dancing partners, I closed my eyes, letting the beat guide me. A set of hands went around my hips, a little too close to my hidden treasure than I liked. I flipped around, seeing some blonde douche-face grinding up on me. I tugged myself out of his grasp and walked back to the bar. He grabbed my arm; there was no warning. I loved to be touched by men, but only when I allowed it.

I closed my fist, meeting it with his face. He groaned in pain, blood coming out of his nose. "You little bitch," he snapped, taking a few steps towards me. I used the training I learned in Quantico, tucking my leg under his calf, pulling him forward which resulted in flipping Mr. Douche Face flat on his back. I put my foot right over his jewels, pressing lightly. "I'm sorry, I don't think I heard that"

"Apologize to the lady, Butch."

I didn't move; my eyes were locked on Butch's, my foot slowly applying pressure to his sensitive area.

"I'm sorry," Butch said. The shithead looked to me, then to whoever was standing behind me. "Are you, really?" I pressed further onto his balls.

"Christ! Yes, I'm sorry!" I removed my foot from his area.

"Butch, don't fuck with me. You won't like what you get."

I spun around, facing Reed. He was maybe two feet behind me. The look on his face made me feel like I was a steak dinner. I felt like I was on fire. Maybe it was the high from kicking a grown man's ass, or maybe it's from the way Reed Michaels was just staring at me.

I walked right past him, going out the front of the bar to my Mustang. Footsteps were right behind me, "Siren, you aren't getting away that easy."

Siren? That was a new one.

I took the key to my car out of my purse, looking over to Reed. "Don't you worry Buttercup, I'll be back." I walked out the door, but I was sure he had followed me.

He had the same look in his eyes. I was dinner, or maybe I was dessert. When a man looks at you with such primal need like that, it's hard not to get aroused. Reed stepped toward me, his arms went around my body, pinning me to my car. He came closer, his chest brushing against my breasts. His left hand held my hip. Holding me so I wouldn't move. His other hand skimmed my skin, starting at my navel, going slowly across my stomach, in between my breasts, to my collarbone and then up my jaw.

I shouldn't have liked the way he was touching me. He was my target. It was my job to find out all his dirty secrets and report them to my handler. Then he would probably be in some deep shit.

But this.

His hands on me were exhilarating.

Reed tilted my head and crushed his lips down onto mine. The kiss was demanding, defining. Surprisingly his lips were soft, not calloused like I'd expected from such a man. Electricity surged through both of our bodies, and I gave in, wrapping my arms around his neck.

I pulled away from him – after all, what the hell was I doing? This is crazy, nuts. I know this is wrong. It's so beyond the parameters of right and wrong.

"You're not getting away that easily, Siren" He repeated, his tone filled with promise, laced with a primal need that I could see in his eyes. His words excited me. I knew everything about Reed Michaels, the notorious MC Prez, yet everything I knew about him was on paper. His words sent fire through my body, he wasn't making a statement but instead with those words it was a promise. But a promise of what? I had a hunch I was about to find out.

"You come here, to my bar, in this sexy as hell get up and expect to leave alone?" He asked, trailing a finger over my outfit. I could feel the heat radiating through my thin jersey top; it's like he was the one fueling my fire, dripping small rounds of gasoline until I'd engulf into flames.

"Yeah, I do" I snapped back, the kiss we shared threw me off kilter, but how dare he expect anything more from me. I'm many things, but a pushover isn't one of them.

"I'm leaving alone," I told him, staring deep into those dangerously dark eyes of his. Those eyes that had me dripping wet the moment I walked into Bubba's. Damn him, and his amazingly good looks. He looked me over, up and down, lingering over my breasts a moment longer than he should have. His smirk confirmed that he wanted me to see him ogling over me.

He took a step closer to me; his chest grazed my breasts yet again, I could feel his breath hitting the top of my forehead. I was nervous – and I'm never fucking nervous. Something about him excited me and terrified me at the same time. He slides his hand under my jaw and tilts my face up, so I'm staring up at him, right into those eyes of his. "Tonight will be the only night you leave alone" I opened my mouth to counter back, to tell him to fuck off, that I'd be leaving alone, however, many times I wanted but suddenly his lips were crushing over mine. I moaned into the kiss, not trying to encourage him but the way those velvety lips came over mine, demanding more from me, wanting more from me – I was toast.

He's a man who takes what he wants, he doesn't ask, he takes and that, well that lights up my fire like nothing else.

Reed slid his greedy hands over me, lifting me into his arms. I didn't object, knowing that I should. I want him as much as he wants me. I heard the click of my car door opening; then I was leaning backward. He turned quickly to shut the car door, leaning over me, staring into my eyes

"So, how's this gonna go Siren? You gonna act like you don't want my cock inside you when I've seen the way you been starin' all night long? Or are you gonna make it easy on both of us and accept the hard fuck imma 'bout to give ya" I should have hated the way he was speaking to me, I don't know what the hell is going on in my mind – I'm so turned on by him.

This is crossing a line, a big red line marked with white ink that says, 'there's no turning back.' Dammit, all to hell, I'm crossing that big line, and I'm going to enjoy it.

"Would you quit your yapping and give me the hard fuck we both want?" I said to him, somehow finding the confidence I didn't know I had. I worked my way to my pants, hooking my fingers under them, sliding them slowly down my legs until I tossed them on the floor. He watched, licking his bottom lip as I entertained him. It was dark, yet still bright enough that I could make out his features.

He didn't speak for a moment; I was wondering if I was even going to get fucked. "Shirt too" I did as he directed, sliding my shirt off, tossing it onto the floor of the car. I had removed my bra before he asked for that as well. When we were kissing like horny teenagers outside of the car, I thought I saw the hunger in his eyes, but that was nothing compared to the crazed animal I see before me right now. He's the lion, and I'm the gazelle.

Without warning, he trailed his hand up my leg and slid two fingers inside me. It should've hurt; it didn't, I was dripping wet for him. The entire night of staring at him, thinking what it would be like if he fucked me, the banter outside my car, he's primed me like no other. "All this for me baby?" He leaned over me, his voice coming out as a husky growl. I didn't speak, debating internally if I should, or if I should just keep my mouth shut.

"I asked you a question. I expect to hear an answer" His voice was firm, demanding. He curled his fingers up against my g-spot and pushed, circling his thumb around my clit. I writhed underneath him, a small whimper escaping my lips. "Answer."

"Yeah, I've been thinking about you fucking me all night" I admitted, staring at him as hungrily as he's been staring at me.

"How am I fucking you?"

"You take me from behind, slamming your cock into my pussy, pulling my hair until I cry out in pleasure" I have no problem admitting what I want. After being with Dick for so long and not having my needs met, I'm not afraid to demand the pleasure that I know I deserve.

He chuckled at my response, crushing his lips down onto mine, working his hand inside my pussy, circling my clit until I was right on edge and the bastard knew it too. He pulled his fingers from me, flipped me over, so my knees were on the leather of the car seat. I heard the foil packet ripping, waiting as he sheathed himself, needing him inside me. I ached for him, for the closeness, for the release that he just denied me. In one swift movement, he was crashing into me. I was drenched for him, but he was huge. A moan slipped past my lips, I clenched onto the leather of the seat, biting my bottom lip, waiting for it to pass. "Give it a minute baby" He whispered, rocking back and forth into me, I could feel myself stretching to accommodate his size with every movement, the initial shock of pain turning into pleasure.

"Fuck, you're the tightest woman I've ever been with" He groaned out, his movements increasing. With every thrust he hit my g-spot, making me cry out in pleasure. He dug his hands into my hip with each thrust. I knew I'd have bruises from how hard he was fucking me. I didn't care. Within minutes I was coming around him, it was so much better than I pictured.

Crossing the line has never felt so damn good.

CHAPTER 3

Elena

The next thing I knew three weeks had passed by, and it was Monday morning, three minutes before 10:00. I'd learned a few things about Skulls Renegade. I'm good at sneaking around, so sneak, I did.

It didn't take long for Reed to take me to the clubhouse. I'd been staying there the past few nights. One time with Reed turned into two, and two turned into ten, and here I am now. There were a few minutes in the day where I was left alone.

Between the sneaking and the chatting with the ladies, I'd learned a bit.

There was a shipment of women coming in, and Daisy told me that it's not what I would think. Apparently, Skulls Renegade would buy women from traffickers and give them new lives. They didn't force them into prostitution. They built lives for them. They saved them from a worse fate.

My phone rang, the caller ID stating it was Kris.

"Hey, Mamacita!" Kris didn't respond to me. "Everything's going great if that's why you're calling."

"Is it, really?" Kris growled, not taking to my cheery attitude at all. "How great is it going? Or is it great because you're sleeping with your target?"

"Oh, so that's why you're in a pissy mood," I replied tartly.

"Damn straight, Elena! What the fuck is wrong with you?!"

"It's given me an in, so don't get shitty until I tell you what I know."

"Spill." I knew Kristie would cave after I had a story to tell. She always did. That was the whole point of my assignment.

"Your informant is blowing bubbles out their ass," I began dramatically. "They don't put women into prostitution. They save them from it. Skulls purchases the women from traffickers. They give them new identities, money, resources to start their lives over."

"You're shitting me."

"Afraid not."

"How do you know this?" Kristie was hooked now, and I felt a small bit triumphant.

"I'm good, that's how. I'll call you in a couple of days." I disconnected the call, clearing the history from the cell. I didn't want any more lectures about my choices now.

I knew it wasn't normal that I was sleeping with my target. Hell, I didn't even know if any of my comrades had ever slept with their targets. I probably wasn't the first, but I felt at least a little guilty.

I felt guilty because I knew what I was there to do: to take down this club. Although, given the information that I had, it may not have had to happen. If they really were helping these women, then the bureau should let them and not take away the small percentage of good just for a tally mark on the board.

I'd worked with too many members of the bureau that were like that, and I sure as hell wouldn't be one of them. If I found the proof that they were helping women, I wouldn't stay on the assignment. It's wrong to help bring down an MC that's trying to help people. Especially when so many others only aim to destroy everything.

I've had my fair share of destruction by another MC.

"Siren!" Reed popped out from his adjoining bathroom. We didn't do much besides having sex, eat and sleep. I was okay with that, though.

"Buttercup," I toyed with him, a small smirk came across my face.

Reed flew out of the bathroom doorway, pinning me down on the bed. "Come shower with me," he growled. He nuzzled his head into my neck, biting softly.

"Are you trying to tell me I stink?" I had to make the guy work for it occasionally, right?

He removed his mouth from my neck, coming right on my face, and he stared me right in my eyes. "No. You smell lovely. Like vanilla and orgasms." I tried not to burst out laughing at his assessment. It was kind of cute for a macho MC prez.

"Vanilla and orgasms? That must be nice."

"You have no idea." He growled again, sounding like a wolf about to attack prey. He pressed his lips down onto mine. He slid his arms under my thighs, repositioning himself, so his hands were cupping my ass. He lifted me into the air, walking us towards the bathroom. While his dominance was admittedly sexy, I had my anxieties.

"Wait!" I screeched, Reed's seen me naked plenty of times, but not under completely fluorescent lighting.

"What's going on?" Reed asked, his gaze was concerning.

"I have scars," I blurted it out without thinking about it. It was probably my biggest insecurity and my biggest reminder about the past I was always running from. "I don't think you've been able to see them, but you will."

"I don't care about scars." He said he didn't, but he would. Once he saw them, he would have to ask me about it.

Reed slid me onto the ground once I was steady, he yanked off my top. "Where are they?"

"My back" I whispered, not even knowing why I felt the need to do so. I'm not particularly ashamed of my past. My past made me who I am. I'm proud of the woman that I am today. I just hate that I had to go through it.

Reed took hold of my shoulders and turned me around, his hand traced along the scar between my shoulder blades. It went all the way down to the bottom of my back.

And that was just the first one.

He found the others, they were a bit smaller, but he did the same thing. Tracing his fingers down the length of them. I had small scars on my inner arm, but nothing like the ones on my back. Reed surprised me, kissing all my scars.

He turned me back around, his hand going to my jaw. His eyes weren't open; he breathed through his nostrils. Finally, when he opened them, I saw the water in his eyes. "Reed." I grazed my hand over his jaw; he was hurt by this. "It's okay, I'm fine," I told him, I would reassure him until he believed me.

I am okay. I am fine.

It took me years to admit that to myself. After someone who is supposed to love you does something like that? Literally, stabs you in the back? It took me a long time to be okay.

"Who did that to you?" He growled it out, his arms pulling me close, he held me against him.

"It doesn't matter. It's in my past, and I'm over it." It was a mantra that ran through my head every day. I also repeated it to Rich, though his concern had been quite different than Reed's.

"Elena, you fucking tell me who did that to you." I yanked away from Reed.

"It doesn't matter because if I ever see him again, I will kill him." It was a promise. The one I intend on keeping. "I'm serious Reed."

I took a breath, gathering my thoughts. Thinking of what I wanted to tell Reed as his...what was I?

His girlfriend? And then there's what I could tell him, as an active agent for the FBI.

Screw the FBI. I hadn't held a promise to them in the whole time I'd been on the assignment anyway.

"That's what this tattoo means." Reed pointed to the tattoo on my hip bone. It read 'Forget what hurt you, but never forget what it taught you.'

I nodded, walking into the bathroom into scorching heat. "Are you coming Buttercup?" I yelled over the strong sounds of the jets, and he popped in behind me.

"I hate when you call me that."

"Lies!" I laughed as he scooped me up into his arms. I wrapped my legs around his torso. His cock was at the entrance of my heated center. "I love where this is going."

He smiled, thrusting into me completely, filling me up. "I thought you would."

I gripped his shoulders as he slammed into me; it wasn't a nice, love making. It was down, dirty fucking; one thing Reed and I were great at. Any sort of sex with Reed was great, but this was heaven.

I felt myself getting close, so I gripped Reed's shoulders, digging my nails into his back. "You're so sexy when you claw at me," Reed grumbled, biting the bottom of my neck. He pulled out, slamming into me again and again.

"Oh my god – Oh – Reed, -yes – Oh," I screamed, my orgasm shooting through me like electricity. Reed released too, slowing his thrusts. He held me in his arms as the aftershocks came to a halt. He slid out of me, helping me stand. "Can you walk after that?" he joked.

"Of course, you're not a sex god." I wasn't sure if I meant that or not.

"Wanna bet?" He scooped me back into his arms, picking back up where we'd just left off.

CHAPTER 4

Elena

It's been another three weeks, and I've figured out I'm smitten for Reed Michaels.

I'm really freaking smitten for him.

I told myself, I'd never, ever, get back into the MC lifestyle, but I could be wrong. I could get back into it for Reed.

I was an MC baby, the daughter of a Prez. I left Austin, leaving behind my past, leaving behind my MC princess title. Princess, ha, more like a captive.

I hadn't been happier to leave that lifestyle behind. It caused me so much pain, and still to this day does. The scars on my back remind me every day.

"What are you in deep thought about?" Jenna asked, coming into Reed's room, which was, in turn, my room, at that point.

"How'd you know?" I scoffed.

"Woman's intuition baby, you'd better be thinking about what you're gonna wear," Jenna chided.

"Wear for what?" I questioned, cocking my head at her in confusion.

"Um, we have another club coming here tonight. We're gonna party. The boys do some business, it's great!" Jenna went through Reed's closet, which I'd basically made my own, she pulled out a few things. "You look hot as fuck in everything, damn you!"

Jenna yanked up a black leather mini skirt and a form-fitting olive tank. "You just like to see me in leather," I teased, raising my eyebrows at her suggestively.

"Doesn't everyone?" Jenna pulled out another one of my outfits, keeping it in her hands. "I'm just gonna borrow this one." She wrinkled her nose in the cute way she sometimes did, her signature move, and wiggled her way out of the room without another word.

**

The party came into full effect, and I sat on the bar top with Jenna and Daisy. Michelle was working at Bubba's tonight, which meant she missed the party, which sucked for her I guessed. But I was glad it meant Daisy was there with me. Secretly, she was my favorite. "How much do you like him?" Daisy said, elbowing me in the side. Reed was sitting on the couch across the room. He looked up to me for a second and smiled. I knew who she was talking about. Daisy always had a way of prying, but then again, it helped me sort out my thoughts in a way I couldn't do on my own.

"Too much. Way too fucking much." I really liked Reed. I mean…. really liked him. He just got me, and we just fit together. It wasn't forced, it was just…us. "I thought I would get a good fuck out of my system and be done with it. But there's no getting Reed out of my system." I smiled at the last bit.

"You're so stinkin' adorable!" Daisy smacked me on the ass, making me hop off the bar.

"Oh, my god, Dais!" I yelled. A loud round of laughter came in from behind me.

The door to the front of the clubhouse creaked open, "I'll be damned Reed you've kept this place the same way your Pop did."

I knew that voice.

I knew it too well.

I wanted to freeze. I wanted to yell, or scream, or maybe even both. I wanted to duck and hide and beg Reed to protect me from him.

Instead, I didn't do a thing. I just stared at Jenna and Daisy. I then quickly scanned the bar area for anything I could use as a weapon.

"Ugh, this guy is such a fucking tool," Daisy groaned, "I'm all about making the men happy, but not this one. No way, Jose."

I listened in on Reed's conversation with him. "Heard you've been with a girl lately, never thought I'd see the day." I heard Reed laugh with him, but

Reed's voice was quiet compared to his. "Is she here? Love to meet the woman who settled you down."

Oh god, no.

"El' are you okay?" Jenna whispered. I shook my head because I was so not. There was no point in hiding it because everyone was about to know who I was.

Escaping Texas didn't do me much good. anymore

My memories came flooding back to me, being fourteen, Mom trying to get us out of there before he came back. We'd almost made it out, almost. He saw us going out the front door. I remembered the look on his face. He was going to kill me. Until she stepped in, he killed her instead. He cut me up that night. All those scars are because of him.

I ran away, made a new life and went to Quantico to hurt people like him.

The fucking devil.

I've avoided seeing my father for ten years. Ten entire years of peace. I knew this day would come, and I was more than capable of doing what I promised.

I didn't have my Glock on me. All the members of the club had theirs except the women. I didn't even bring my certified piece, but that would have blown my cover. If I even had a cover at this point.

"Firecracker, is that you?" I forgot there was a god damned mirror in front of the bar. He could see my image clear as day. I turned around, facing the beast, the monster that created me. Everyone in the room turned their direction to me. Jimmy Jacobson moved towards me. I looked for a gun, one I could reach, I didn't find it.

Seamus came up to the left of me, and then Max came on my other side. I'd never been more thankful for some backup. Did I look as terrified as I felt? Or did Reed send them both a silent signal?

"Shit! It is you. Been a long time sweet cheeks." My father clapped his hands together. The sound was sickening and instantly set my blood boiling. Was he really going to stand there and play nice?

"Not long enough," I growled back, and Reed's eyes were glued to mine. He was watching my reaction. He did send his guys over to me. Thank god, this man knew me so well even after this brief time that he could tell something was wrong.

He turned around the room. "Do any of you have an idea who she is?!" He grinned from ear to ear. "I'll take that as a no. Elena is my daughter." Gasps filled the room, "My prestigious daughter. She is the heiress to the Vipers MC. How funny is it that she abandons the lifestyle, and now she's here?"

He reminded me of Neagan from The Walking Dead. He was just as nasty. He looked to Reed. "So, my whore of a daughter is the one who locked you down?" He laughed, and Reed tightened his jaw in response. Jimmy redirected his attention back to me, taking a couple steps towards me.

"Come at me. I fucking dare you."

"Really now?" Jimmy challenged me, taking a step towards me. I didn't think; I took Seamus' Glock out of the holster, turned the safety off and shot him in both kneecaps with exact precision. He fell to the floor, and the motherfucker laughed.

I flipped the safety back on, handing it to Seamus. "Sorry, but not really." Seamus nodded at me. Reed continued to stare at me, almost in disbelief. I didn't regret what I did. They would believe what they wanted to, but this was personal.

I walked up to my father, "I promised you I'd end this, and I will, but not yet. I want you to suffer just like we did. I want to watch the life go out of your eyes, you sick fuck." I walked out the front of the clubhouse, feeling the stare of everyone on my back.

Once that cool Tennessee air hit me, I felt like I could finally breathe. I stood next to one of the posts, gripping my hand around it. If the wind blew in the wrong direction, I knew I would fall over.

I'd expected some sort of reunion with my father. Part of me craved the day I would see him, the day I could repay all the pain that he caused my mother and me. What I didn't expect, was to be caught off guard by him.

"Elena." Reed's voice was stern, but I didn't even look back. Tears were sliding down my face. It wasn't because I was guilty, or sad, or even angry. I was terrified.

I was terrified that I was going to lose Reed.

He stood behind me for a moment; he put his hand on my shoulder, I jumped at the contact. "S-sorry."

He came around the front of me, cupping my face. He wiped the tears away, just letting me silently cry. "I've got you, baby. I've got you." And he did. He had me.

"Prez, what we doin' with him?" Someone asked Reed, and he mumbled something about being back inside in a bit. He kept me close to him, gently caressing me. "Your father gave you the scars." It was a statement, and true.

"Yes."

I walked out of his grip since I was going to tell him everything, I needed to do it on my own. I couldn't have him comforting me through it. "My father had always beat my mother and I, the first time I remembered it, I was…four I think? When I was fourteen, we'd planned to leave. We had two duffle bags packed, and we were leaving that night. We timed it. He normally came home around ten. If anyone had seen us leave early, they would've told him. So, we waited, we waited until the Prospect who watched our house left. Only, we didn't know he would come home early that night. He caught us, he dragged me across the kitchen and marked me."

I took in a breath, the tears came down my face, and I looked right into Reed's eyes. "My mom, she pleaded with him for it to be her, to not kill me. I thought I was going to die that night, and when she…I knew he would kill her. He wasn't just going to mark her, or punish her, or do whatever else the twisted fuck thought he could do. She knew she was going to die. She kept telling me 'It will be okay, stay strong, you can do this El'"

"He brought out a baseball bat from the garage, tied her up to a chair in our kitchen and beat her to death. He made me watch." I felt sick talking about it. "I trained, and trained so I could put men like him in one place, the ground." He didn't ask me about my marksmanship, but he would. It would come up, and I knew that much. Not many can make shots like that.

One of my father's men came out. It was Dmitri, his VP.

"Boss, what do you want us to do with him?" Reed looked to Dmitri and began to speak.

"Not you – her."

"I guess you just inherited an MC," Reed said, and Dmitri nodded in confirmation. "I've looked for you, young blood. It's time we have the change that we need."

"Dmitri, I can't…" I'd known Dmitri since I was a child. He had been at my father's side for as long as I could remember. When he interrupted me, I wasn't surprised. He said whatever the hell he wants to.

"Elena, you can and you will. Without you, we don't have a club. He's done fucked up things. More fucked up than good, but we have people depending on us. We have Old Ladies and kids. We can't just stop."

I chewed on his words for a moment, knowing he was right. As much as I had always wanted to walk away and be done with it, my actions had just committed me to a whole new slew of outlaws that needed my protection as much as the ones I have grown to love over the last few weeks. But if I was going to be Prez of the sinister MC group my devil of a father had run for so many years, it was going to be on my fucking terms.

"One condition, everything illegal stops. Everything, Dmitri."

He nodded, "I'll get started on it."

Things just got more complicated. I was working with the FBI, and now I had an MC all my own. A soap opera writer couldn't come up with this shit.

It was going to make me just as much of a target as Reed. I needed to figure something out fast; it was only going to get more and more complicated.

I needed to talk to Kris, as soon as possible.

CHAPTER 5

Elena

I woke up in Reed's arms; he was still in bed. Normally, he would be up at the crack of dawn. I knew last night took a toll on both of us.

I reached over the side of the bed, pulling out my burner phone, knowing there was no better moment than the present to start working things out with the FBI. The sooner things were sorted out, the safer myself and everyone I cared for would be.

To: Kris

I need to see you ASAP. When can you get here?

Not even a minute later, she texted me back.

From: Kris

6 hrs. Where?

To: Kris

Bubbas, call me when you're close.

Reed rolled over, pulling me back against him. "Turn the damn phone off, babe." I turned around to face him, brushing my hand across his face. I loved touching his face. I loved waking up with him in bed. I loved him. I hadn't told him that yet, though.

"What are you thinking so hard about?" he asked, reading me once again. He had become an expert at that one.

"Nothing." I tried to play it off, but I doubted he bought it.

He laughed at me, opening his eyes. "I can sense when you're doing the squishy face, and you were squishy facing it."

"You know me so well," I said. I sat up on the bed, Indian style. He did know me, but he didn't. I didn't alter my cover story when I came here. Everything I'd ever said to him had been the truth. Minus the fact that I worked for the FBI.

Yeah, minus that.

"I do, and don't you forget it." He slapped my ass. "Ouch!" I yelled, but he just smiled at me, that devilish smile that I'd come to adore. Reed shot up, pulling me onto his lap. He slid his hand underneath my shorts, rubbing the reddened flesh. With his other hand, he went under the pathetic excuse of a shirt I had on. It had so many holes in it; it could count as lingerie from Victoria's Secret. He stopped at my breast, rubbing his thumb over my erect nipple. Reed put his mouth over the other, sucking me into his mouth.

"Mmmm, now this is an enjoyable way to wake up." He mumbled something against my breast that I couldn't make it out. He kept sucking and pinching. "Can we move this along?" I groaned.

Reed was such a tease, and I hated it. I loved it when we have hours to go on, but when we had like an hour before we both had to be up, I hated it even more.

I suddenly flew back against the bed, he ripped my shirt in half, exposing my body. "So, fucking beautiful."

Reed came back down to me, biting my nipple with his teeth. He grabbed my shorts and panties, tearing them down my legs onto the floor below us. His hands slid between my folds, showing him how wet I was, how eager I was for him to be inside me.

"Reeeeeeed," I groaned as he came up from my breast, smirking wildly. "There will be plenty of time for that later, precious."

"I want you to fuck me." I was stern, promising in my tone. I wasn't playing around, I was horned up, and I needed his dick inside me. His head went to my neck. His playful biting continued, for a few minutes I let it happen, his fingertips glided up my body. Reed made me feel beautiful, like the sexiest woman on the planet.

His thumb brushed against my clit, causing me to squirm instantly. "Anxious, are we?"

"Reed, fuck me or get out!" I don't think he knew how serious I was. I was tired of the teasing. I wanted him to be inside me. It wasn't just because I was horned up. I loved the connection we had, and when we had sex, it intensified so much.

"Ultimatums?" Reed got off the bed and walked towards the bathroom. He cocked his head back. "I don't like ultimatums, baby."

"I don't like getting teased!" I growled out. "Get over here!" I sat up on the bed, he didn't move, he just stared at me. He would come, in more ways than one.

I knew how he operated.

I slid my legs open, giving him a gracious view of my waxed pussy. He could pretend he didn't want it as much as I did, but he did. I could see right through his bullshit, and I was giving him an invitation he had to take. "I'm not asking." I'm demanding. I'm telling. In all seriousness, he'd better get over here, or he wouldn't be getting laid for a week.

Reed came to me. His tree trunk arms lifted me into the air, he slid into me, lifting me up and down on his cock like he's at the gym lifting weights. He put his mouth over my breast, biting down on my nipple. I screamed in ecstasy when the first orgasm came, and then the second and by the third he had me on my stomach on our bed, pounding into me from behind. "Reed – Oh – Reed," I moaned, and he smacked my ass hard. At first, it hurt, but then it felt amazing, he smacked my other cheek as he slammed into me. I fell prisoner to the best orgasm of my entire life. I saw stars. The sky changed to purple.

I'm was truly in heaven.

He stopped when his orgasm came, and he stayed inside me for a minute, then slid out, holding me against him. "That was…amazing," I breathed.

"Damn fucking straight." Reed kissed the top of my head, his hand grazed up and down my arm sweetly.

***

Six hours felt like six entire days, and I was antsy the entire afternoon. It was ten minutes before the six hours were up, and I went back into Reed's and my room and slipped into a black lace bodysuit. I paired it with a pair of black jeggings and of course black heels.

I looked in the mirror. I looked hot.

"Damn, chicka! Where're you off to?" Michelle said. Every head turned in the room to her comment. I wanted to chuckle; half the men had their mouths open.

"You guys might want to pick your jaws up from off the floor before Reed comes in," I warned.

They shut their mouths just Reed came walking in through the front door of the clubhouse. Now his jaw was on the floor, "Where the hell are you going dressed like that? Besides our bedroom." The guys in the clubhouse laughed, as did some of the women.

He was cute. Too bad I didn't like cute.

I walked towards him, "I'm going to Bubba's. My best friend is coming into town."

"You're not going alone." Reed was firm, his eyes glancing over my outfit. I leaned up to his ear and whispered: "I'll make it up to you later, you can see my entire ensemble."

"No. You aren't going alone. I'm coming with you."

"No!" I just made an ass of myself. "No, I mean...she doesn't know that, uh...I'm seeing anyone."

"Perfect, a great time for introductions. Who else is coming?" He shouted it to the group of men, a few turned and exited on their bikes. Reed grabbed my hand. I thought we were going to my Mustang. Instead, he brought me up to his bike, "Uh…Reed?"

He laughed at me, sliding his jacket off, and he put it on me, zipping it up completely. He handed me a helmet, securing it for me. "I'm gonna get on, and you're just gonna hop on behind me, and hold tight, okay?" I nodded to his instructions. I'd never ridden with him or anyone for that matter. Sure enough, he got on, and I somehow managed to get on behind him. I held onto him for dear life, and we were off.

The ride to Bubba's was short, mainly because Reed flew like the fucking devil up the roads. I spotted the unmarked car I knew Kristie was in, but

I couldn't see her inside, so I took Reed's help getting off the bike and looked for the woman I knew would stand out. She was sitting at the bar, Max was next to her, probably hitting on her. Kristie is fucking hot, with a capital H. She's petite, with a curvy body and long blonde hair.

"Kris!" I yelled, waving at her. She seemed relieved at first until she saw Reed's arm around me. I turned, facing him. "Babe, can I talk to her first, and then I'll come find you?" He nodded, kissing me on the lips.

I smiled as he walked away, then approached Kristie. "Max, get lost." I tapped him on the shoulder. He did as I said, and I slid up next to Kris. "You invited me to their biker bar?" She was annoyed, but at least it was here and not some preppy ass restaurant like we had in Cincinnati.

"What the fuck is going on El'?" Kristie was annoyed, maybe even pissed.

"Some things have changed. Major things." I went through the process of telling her about my father, about me inheriting the club. Even a little bit about Reed.

"So, you're head over heels for him?" she asked. I suppose it was obvious. Why else would I have risked all I had already?

"Yep." There was no hesitation in my voice. I was head over heels for him. He was amazing. "I've got it bad. Kris, I need to re-negotiate things. It's different now."

"I was afraid that was coming up." She was rolling her eyes at me as my handler, but as my best friend, I knew she was happy.

"I want immunity for everyone affiliated with Skulls Renegade MC and Vipers MC. I can continue to work for the bureau with Vipers, but I don't want Skulls Renegade to have any part of it. They aren't doing anything dirty, Kris, they don't deserve it."

"Fine. Immunity, for you all. But you'd better keep your end of the deal. I need names. I need the players that are shipping these girls around."

"You've got it, but I'm buying the women as they come in, from Vipers MC. I'm getting a program up like Reed has. I will not let these women be sold into worse fates, not when I can do something about it." Kris nodded at me, telling me she was on board. "Now, do you want to meet my boyfriend?" I grinned from ear to ear.

"I can't believe you found an MC man. I cannot fucking believe it."

"Well, believe it, darling, because it's happened!" I scooted off my barstool until I found Reed, he was chatting with Seamus. "Come, pass the friend test," I joked, Seamus laughed his ass off, Reed took my hand.

We walked up to Kris, and Reed was getting nervous. "Reed, this is my best friend, Kristie. Kristie, this is Reed." They both exchanged hello's, after that it wasn't so bad.

"Who's the big guy who keeps staring at us?" Kris asked, and I turned on Reed's lap and looked at Seamus. "That's Seamus, and he's not looking at us. He's looking at you."

"Like the WWE wrestler?"

I died laughing. Reed joined in. "El' said the same thing when she met him," he explained. "I'm surprised she even watched WWE."

"Um, WWE is amazing. Muscular men in latex, it's practically porn. Ask any woman why they watch WWE, they will tell you the same thing."

"Daisy! Why do you watch WWE?" Reed yelled over the bar. She giggled and winked.

"For the hot ass men in latex!"

"Point proved. Checkmate bitch," I said smugly. We all sat at the bar for the next two hours eating and drinking.

"Is she always like this?" Reed asked Kristie in a teasing tone.

"Hey, you can't return her now. She's all yours," Kris laughed, I did too.

"Aw! She likes you!"

"Well, I've got to get back to Ohio. Keep me up to date, and Mondays, remember." I saluted Kris as she walked through the doors.

"You know who I'd love to see in some latex?" I put on my super sexy voice, whispering into his ear.

"Hell fucking no. No matter what you do, I will never fucking do that."

"But I'm supposed to get in latex, and leather, and things like this?" I moved my hand over my lace, see-through bodysuit.

Reed growled at me, "Woman, you're the devil."

"Then you're a sinner." I crushed my lips down onto his, moving my hands up into his hair as he planted his hands on my ass. I heard woop woop's coming from the room. "I think we've got an audience," I muttered. He smiled at me, returning to our kiss.

I pulled away when I couldn't breathe anymore, "I love your kisses."

Reed tightened his grip around me, biting down on my neck. "Reed," I growled, he moved his lips up my neck, pressing along my jawline. The doorway opened, displaying a few men from my MC and a few guys who I didn't recognize.

"I'll be back." Reed slid me down on the barstool. Daisy came trotting up from behind the bar.

"Damn girl, he is packing on the PDA with you."

"Mhm. I don't mind it though." And I truly didn't.

"Funny, a few months ago, you were in this exact seat, and he was over there. I love how you two turned out."

"Awww, thanks, Mom!" Daisy smacked me with a wet towel, "More vodka!" She brought me a couple shots. I took one back. Daisy met every shot

I took with one of her own. She went back behind the bar when a man I didn't recognize spoke to me.

"Irish, you're looking hot tonight." Irish? What is he, twelve? I don't know him, "I think you're talking to the wrong person."

"Oh no, I'm talking to the right woman. I'm just wondering if the carpet matches the curtains." Oh, my god. Thank god, I could keep a poker face, that was something I wasn't expecting. Mr. Sexy Talk put his hand on my hip and started to slide it around me. I picked his arm up, moving it off me. "You, keep your hands to yourself."

"Why, love? There's no patch on your back. I don't see your man around here. Are you claimed? You someone's Old Lady?"

"My man is around here, a matter of fact. That's him." I shifted my eyes to Reed aggressively walking up to me

"Kyle, leave my Old Lady alone."

"Can't blame me, she's a nice piece. Where's her cut?" Kyle was stepping on Reed's toes, I didn't know Kyle, but from the way Reed was acting, they weren't on the best of terms. "At home."

"Hmpf" Kyle muttered, he stared me up and down then looked back to Reed. "You scored a Unicorn, how'd you manage that, Brother?"

Daisy came back over to us. She stared at Kyle. "What the fuck are you doing here?! Get out!"

Daisy picked up a shot of vodka and threw it on him.

"I can remember a time I made you that wet."

"Reed, get your asshole of a brother out of here before I find a knife and do it myself!"

"I'll see you in the clubhouse." Kyle smacked Reed's shoulder. "I'll see you later baby," Daisy responded by flipping him the bird. He walked out the front of the bar.

"I didn't know you had a brother." Reed didn't respond to me, he just grabbed me, keeping his arm wrapped around my waist.

"You don't walk around in the house unless I'm with you, or one of the other brothers are there. Got me?"

"What?" Is this because his brother was here? "Reed, what the hell?"

"He's my evil twin. Evil being the primary word there, babe. Just do it, for me." I caved and accepted his terms, "Let's go home."

Reed flew through the mountains until we came right into the district of Gainesville, he sped up, completely ignoring the speeding signs. I wasn't surprised when I saw some blue coming up in his mirrors. "Shit," he growled, little did he know I could make this go away.

Reed slowed down along the shoulder. The officer came up to us. "I'm going to handle this, so just be quiet," I told Reed, the officer was right next to us.

"Officer, I'm just going to pull out my identification from my purse. Okay?"

"Miss, I don't need to see your identification. I need the driver's."

"Sir, I believe you want to see mine." He nodded to me. I grabbed my federal ID issued by the bureau and handed it to him. He flipped it open, looking at me and then my ID. I slid my helmet off, "Ah. Agent Johnson, my apologies."

"It's perfectly fine." He handed me my ID and walked back to his car, I slid it back into my purse, put my helmet back on and tightened my arm around Reed.

"What was that?"

"I'll tell you when we get home."

Chapter 6

Elena

In my mind, I began to prepare whatever story I was going to feed to Reed. Obviously, it would have to consist of a piece of the truth. He wasn't going to buy an outright lie at this point. But to protect my job as well as to protect him, I had to try and keep information to a minimum. I was head over heels for the man that was supposed to be my target, but I couldn't help but regret my poor, reckless choice to sleep with the enemy at that moment.

Reed looked at me expectantly as I paced in front of our bed. He didn't say anything, though, and chose to be patient with me. He was an awfully good man for the Prez of an MC. "Okay, Reed, you're going to have to trust me on this. I can't tell you everything for my protection and yours. All of this could blow up in my face if I divulge it all." I sat down on the bed next to him, hoping he wasn't about to kick me out of his bed and his life. Not only would it ruin my career, but it would also break my heart.

"Damn, Siren. This is serious, isn't it?" he asked me, scratching his head.

I nodded, taking a deep breath. "My name, the story about my Mom and Dad, all that about my ex, it was the truth." I wanted to make that clear first. I had never specifically lied to Reed. My cover was basically blown the moment I got here, but nobody suspected I had a cover, to begin with.

"I can see that. Nobody makes up that shit about their father. Plus, I've met the ass more than once. It was clear he had done something to you." I placed my hand on Reed's knee and smiled up at him. He was the opposite of my asshole ex and the opposite of any man I thought I would fall for. Yet, here I was worried he would reject me for who I was. "So, how about ya tell me why you were able to get us out of that back there with just an id?"

I sighed, knowing it was time to let it all out. Well, as much of it as I could. "Like I said, Reed. I can't tell you all of it. What I can tell you is that I didn't just show up here by accident and that my job affords me quite a few privileges. Please, don't make me put anyone here in danger by telling you more than that," I begged of him, knowing he would be able to glean enough from those two statements. He would at least realize I was with the government or law enforcement somehow.

"I don't like it one bit, Siren." Reed shook his head, and I felt my stomach threaten to drop out my ass. "But it sure is fucking adorable that you are trying to protect me." A smile broke on Reed's face, and he pulled me down onto the bed, planting his lips on mine. I felt like I had just dodged a bullet there. Reed was on board still, at least for now.

Man, was this assignment getting complicated. It was just another thing I would probably have to warn my handler about. But for now, I wanted to enjoy my time with Reed before his brother came sticking his rude ass nose around our business again.

I let Reed take off my clothes, throwing them into a forgotten pile on the floor. I loved the way he made me feel both beautiful and wild. Dick had been so damn controlled in the bedroom, and that was when I even got to spend that kind of time with him. He had made me feel so buttoned up and boring. Reed was so far from those things with his crazy driving, sharp tongue, and incredibly hot and tan body covered in tats. He was this woman's wet dream.

Reed's hands slid all over my body as his tongue lapped up the flavor of my salty skin. "Fuck, you taste so good, Siren. I can't believe I get to savor you every day."

I smiled to myself and let out a small moan at his comment as his hand found that warm, throbbing spot between my legs that he knew just what to do with.

"I can't believe I get to be in your bed every day," I told him in response as his fingers slid inside me, silencing my words as pleasure traveled up my spine.

If only I could keep this part of my job up forever and never worry about the rest of what lay ahead, but the reality was I was the Prez of an MC now and involved with the Prez of another. There was danger lurking at every corner from the bureau, the members, and the cartel that I had to dive in head first as soon as I could. On top of that, Jimmy was still waiting for me to do something about him.

My body shook under Reed's touch, and I rocked my hips against his hand. At least, for now, I could hide out in Reed's bedroom and let him ravage my body. I could save the rest for later.

CHAPTER 7

Elena

I let the rest of the day go by that way; just me and Reed, letting him know that the next day we'd be dealing with Jimmy together. We were going to send his ass straight to hell as a team.

I had lost track of time when Reed suddenly got up as if he had remembered something. He began rummaging in his small closet and pulled something out, bringing it straight to me. It took me a moment to realize what it was, and my mind shot back to what he'd told his asshole brother who'd hit on me earlier in the day. I had no idea how he would have gotten such a thing without me knowing about it, but there it was. A leather jacket. It was my cut.

"I wasn't lyin' when I told Kyle I had your cut here. You're my girl, babe. My ride or die. I want every motherfucker out there to know that you're mine, you're the Ol' Lady of Skulls Renegade MC," he told me with his broadest smile. It meant so many things, what he was doing and saying, and my head swam.

Being an Ol' Lady is the equivalent of an engagement in an MC, or at least very close. That scared me to death. I loved Reed, and I wanted to be his Ol' Lady, but I didn't want to be engaged. Not yet. I had just gotten out of an engagement that ended in the worst way possible, or close to it. I suppose Richard didn't die on me. Just his love did.

Reed pulled the cut out in front of me, and I was amazed when I saw the back of the jacket. The emblem was different than anything else I'd ever seen on a cut before. Instead of it being a skull, for Skulls Renegade MC, it was half a skull and half a viper; showing my affiliation with both clubs. On the front, my patch read 'Prez – VMC' and 'Ol' Lady Prez – SRMC.'

"Reed..." I could cry. It was so perfect. There was no way I could turn him down now. "Thank you. Thank you so damned much." I wrapped my arms around him, and he held me close just the way I liked.

"Anything for you baby." And when he said it like that, the cut clutched between us, I believed him. Maybe it really didn't matter that I was an FBI agent after all; at least not to him.

***

We'd had a full night of life changing sex. And I know I'd told myself that a million times since meeting Reed, but I'd never had anything better. Sex with Reed just kept getting better. I couldn't believe I had enjoyed sex with Richard because this was out of this world. What had I been missing all those years?

Groggily, as the morning came along, I looked over and smiled euphorically. Reed was sleeping in with me. He was laying on his back, and I wrapped my arm around his torso. My head was lying on his chest, going up and down with his smooth breathing. He still wasn't awake yet, and I wasn't about to be the one to disturb him. I liked him just the way he was for now.

A flash of light came into our room, breaking the nice moment. I cringed, and I groaned when the light got brighter. It suddenly all turned off, and I was brave and opened my eyes. Who was the hell disturbing us like that?

I saw Kyle, staring at us. "Oh, my god!" I shrieked, causing Reed to shoot up out of bed. "What, what's the – "

"What the fuck are you doing in here!?" Reed brought the duvet up over my shoulders so that I was covered completely. Evidently, Reed had given the right advice about being around his brother. We were both in our birthday suits, and I'm sure he enjoyed the view.

"Get out!" I yelled. Kyle just smirked, but he did as I told him. He left.

Reed got out of bed and started sliding on his tight, black pants. "Reed, please just lock the door and come back to bed," I pleaded, wanting a few more moments of peace before I had to face the fateful day ahead of me.

"Sorry *Siren*, but I'm too worked up for that."

"Reeeeeeeed," I whined. He shot a warning glare back to me.

"Don't whine to me, babe. You sleep, and then get up and wear that cut today. I'll see you in a bit." He kissed my forehead. "We need to figure out what exactly we're doing with Jimmy today."

Ugh, that reminder. I almost forgot about him. For once in my life, I wish I'd forgotten about him. It would have been fucking great. I rolled out of bed and headed towards the bathroom. I turned on the shower, and it was steaming hot; just the way I liked it best.

I did as Reed said, taking my time while he did whatever it was he was going to do to deal with that evil twin of his. How could such an amazing man be so closely related to that dick?

I put on the cut over my clothes and went out to the living area in the clubhouse. Daisy stood next to the coffee pot, pouring herself a cup. "Can I get one too?" I asked, feeling like I could use several to fuel my day.

Daisy jumped, then turned around to face me. She looked like crap, and her eyes were swollen. She'd been crying all night, or maybe fell asleep crying? I'd been that girl too many times, and that's what she was today. I had to get to the bottom of why my best friend in that place was so down in the mouth. It wasn't like Daisy at all to be anything but cheerful.

"Dais' what's wrong?" She poured me a cup of coffee without a response. When she handed it to me, I pressed it to my lips, taking a sip of the warm liquid. I took a glance around the room. Luckily, it was just Daisy and me for now. Reed must have taken Kyle elsewhere to deal with him. "Is this about Kyle?" I asked more quietly.

"Sometimes I hate how observant you are." She took a pull of her own coffee and stared at me right in the eyes. Her eyes were brimming with tears. "Him coming back here just brought up a lot of old shit." Daisy took a deep breath. "He has the fuckin' nerve, coming back here after he just…left."

"It was a bad breakup?" Everything I'd known from the information I'd gathered pointed to that.

Daisy just laughed at me. "I don't even think ya can classify it as a breakup. There was no breakup;

he just fuckin' left." She inserted quotations with her fingers for the word "break up."

"I never stopped loving him, the fuckin asshole. I was fine. I was totally fuckin' fine with him being gone and it being what it was. Now he just shows up here? What the hell does he want? He gave the damn club away to Reed cuz he wanted none of it." Daisy threw her hands in the air in frustration before leaning over the counter, looking a bit defeated. "Damn it! I was fine. I dealt with my shit and now – now it's all comin' back to me." She shivered talking about it, and I put my coffee on the counter and took her into a strong embrace. Daisy sobbed, her tears sliding over my shirt. "I can't b-be strong a-all the fuckin' t-time. I just can't, Elena."

"You don't have to baby girl. I've gotcha." In the last few weeks since I'd been there, I'd never seen Daisy cry, not even once. She's a tough chick. Something must have gone horribly wrong if she was crying like this. I hoped that Reed got Kyle good for the both of us.

***

After I had left Daisy in her room, I went in search of Reed. I was alone, which he specifically said he didn't want. There wasn't anyone in the club. Literally, no one was here. Odd much? But then again, Reed and Kyle were probably together. So, I was fine, right?

From my discussions with Reed over the past day, I had assumed that my father was still alive.

Both MCs were waiting on me to execute an official order or finish the job myself. Though, I figured the man probably had it bad where they were keeping him.

With the single thought of him, my childhood memories came back to me in a flash. Shit. He'd taken so much from my mother and from me. In the end, he took her from me. That was something I was never going to be able to forgive him for.

No matter how much I could try, I never would. Not after everything. So, if that made me a bad person, so fuckin' be it.

When I was, little I used to imagine that I had a normal dad. You know what I'm talking about; one of the dads who take you to soccer, to the movies. It was a beautiful imagination; my father was never like that. When my friend Sophie got presents, I got slaps to the face. And that was on a good day.

I knocked softly on Reed's office door, then opened it. Reed was behind the desk, wearing a look that could kill hundreds staring at his brother. As I suspected, he had pulled him away to deal with him, but I kind of wished there were more physical dealings going on than glaring.

"You need to fix your shit with Daisy," I told him point blank.

Kyle turned to me as I came in with the most annoying shit-eating grin on his lousy face, "Mornin' Irish."

CHAPTER 8

Reed

I watched as my new Ol' Lady walked up to my asshole evil twin and slapped him hard across the face. I couldn't help but smirk. She was so hot when she was in a bad mood like that, and Kyle knew damn well he deserved it. "If I were you I'd watch your damn mouth around my Ol' Lady," I warned him, nodding to the fiery look on Elena's face.

Kyle looked at her more closely, finally noticing the cut now. "What the hell kind of cut is that?" he asked, surveying the unique patch I had specially made for my beautiful Siren. She was my Ol' Lady and the Prez of another powerful MC she inherited from her dirtbag father.

"I'm his Ol' Lady, but I'm also the Prez of the Vipers. Pretty sure that's why he said to watch your damn mouth and listen to me. Like I said, you need to fix your shit with Daisy. I've never seen her like this, and I have half a mind to punch you in the damn balls right now for being such a piece of shit. But you're Reed's brother, so I'm going to give you one more fucking chance to act the right way." Damn, Siren was pissed good today. It was going to be a great day to wipe Jimmy off the face of the earth, then. And then they could take it back to the bedroom and celebrate.

I felt myself getting hard just thinking about it and shifted in my seat. "Do what she says if you wanna stay here, bro. I don't know why the hell you're here, and I have more important things to do right now than care. But you dropped this MC in my lap and disappeared, so you have no say any longer. And if you're going to be here, you're not going to be making my members cry or pissing off my Ol' Lady, is that clear?" I glared daggers at him, hoping I got through to the guy.

Brother or not, I never had understood him. But he had been my father's right-hand man and the natural go to lead the Skulls Renegade MC. Kyle dropped it in my lap a year after getting it and walked the fuck out if our lives.

Kyle nodded and got up, getting in Elena's face. I stood up with my fists balled up, ready to rearrange his fuckin' face, but all he said to her was, "Sure thing, Irish," before walking out into the bar, calling for Daisy.

I gave a one-sided smirk before coming out from behind my desk and heading straight for my Ol' Lady. Man, I never thought I was going to say that about any woman. Sure, I had been with plenty of chicks looking to get some from a Prez, but there had never been any woman that I thought could stand by my side. But my siren was damn tough as nails, and I knew it from the moment she walked into that bar like she owned the place that she was bound to be mine.

I pushed Elena against the wall and planted one on her, letting my hand enjoy her thick thigh for a moment before pulling away. We couldn't get lost in each other just yet. There was some business to take care of. "Good morning, Siren. I see you're in a mood. Are you ready to put that to use on Jimmy?"

Instead of anger, I saw her face visibly droop and knew that she was still haunted by that motherfucker's existence. And she was no killer, but I was sure that the death of this asshole was going to turn her life around more than she could even imagine. And it was going to satisfy my burning hatred for a man I should have never had dealings with. It made me fuckin sick that this man tortured the woman I loved when she was just a child and dared to kill her own mother in front of her. There was a special place in hell for bastards like that, and he was going to figure that out real soon.

"I don't see any reason to wait any longer. Where are they keeping him?" she asked. Little did she know he had been holed up in the basement with 24/7 guard this whole time. That place was a padded-up torture chamber. Not even one of us above ground could hear him scream.

"Grab your Glock and follow me," I told her, leading her past the bedroom to grab the gun she'd kept hidden since she got there. I'd had my slight suspicions about her before; I wasn't as stupid as people sometimes took me for. But it did take me by fuckin' surprise when she used a badge to get us out of a ticket. She was something else.

She tucked it away in the pocket of her cut, and I held my hand out to her. We were going to do this together, just the way we would do everything from now on. We were going to be unstoppable as the Prez and Ol' Lady of Skulls Renegade MC.

There was a little-known entrance into the basement through the laundry area; just a small little hole in the floor with some stairs leading down into the dark. But as we descended this time, it was lit up by the dim lightbulb swinging free in the very center of the room.

The basement wasn't much to speak of; just concrete and a water heater. We had a few pieces of junk down there. Otherwise, it was meant for exactly the purpose we were using it for now; holding prisoners. Seamus, Enzo, and Dmitri were all down there, taking a couple of lame shots at the old man who looked worse for the wear. Other than the shit eating grin he shot through his bloodied mouth at Elena, there was nothing recognizable about him. I had made sure he had been fed nothing but gruel and that he was being kept quiet and weak down there until Elena was ready.

"Well, well, well. If it isn't my little bitch of a daughter. Have you come to bust out my knee caps again, or are you here to be the little weakling you always were and set me free?" he asked, spitting up blood the whole time. I noticed his teeth had recently been kicked in.

I went straight to the corner for a baseball bat and pulled out my own gun to train on him. "Leave the three of us the fuck alone now, guys. He's all ours. Thanks. Oh, and Enzo, Seamus, keep a close, damn eye on Kyle, would ya?" The two men nodded, keeping their weapons trained on Jimmy until they were halfway up the stairs.

"I'm here to watch the light go out of your fuckin eyes for what you did to Mom," she told him point blank with gritted teeth. "I'm here to watch you pay."

Jimmy spit more blood and pus out at Elena, and I went at him with the bat. I cracked it only lightly against his shoulder. "I didn't hit you any fuckin harder because I am pissed off, asshole. This is not going to be a fast job today, Jimmy. You see, it takes the worst sort of coward to shoot his own wife in front of their children and even more so to beat the shit out of an innocent little girl.

Well, that little girl grew up to be my Ol' Lady, and I'll be damned if anyone hurts my Ol' Lady and lives to tell the tale." I was drooling with anger at this point, staring down evil incarnate as I swung the bat again, going for his already banged up knees.

"Get the fuck up!" I screamed at him as he let himself fall over, looking more like an injured Santa Claus than the beast he had pretended to be for so long. But I knew his rep well enough to know that he was just a shithead hiding behind his MC.

He followed my directions, but he did so, laughing maniacally through the pain.

"Stop fuckin' laughin'."

He was driving me insane, and it took all my willpower not just to end him right there. Instead, a cracked one across his other shoulder, snapping the bone. Jimmy faltered and screamed in agony for a moment, and I glanced at Elena, making sure she saw his pain. She deserved that.

But then the motherfucker got back up to his knees like the sick cockroach he was and spoke his last. "I see how my little whore worked her way into your bed. You talk too damn much, Reed. Your father or brother would never have let an FBI agent in their midst." Reed glanced back at Elena for a moment as her eyes went wide. "That's right little baby, I've known for years that you're a fuckin government snitch. I should've popped one right in your skull when I had the chance."

Elena didn't hesitate, pulling out her Glock and getting him point blank between the eyes. He fell over with a thud, bleeding out onto the concrete. Elena dropped her piece as she sank to the ground shaking.

Obviously, we had some shit to clear up, but first, she needed me. I wrapped my arms around her and rocked her back and forth until the shaking turned to tears. "He's fuckin dead, Reed. He's gone."

"I know, babe. It's all over. He only has the devil to torture now."

CHAPTER 9

Elena

I paced back and forth in the Cincinnati hotel room that Reed and I had been holed up in the last 24-hours awaiting the phone call from the bureau. After the death of Jimmy and the way he had just thrown around the information about me being an agent, I knew I couldn't fuck around anymore. Things were getting too deep and dangerous for me not to cut an official deal with the FBI for myself as well as the now two MCs involved. Kristie had urged me to come to Cincinnati immediately to square things away with her boss. Reed insisted, even after learning who I was, that he come with me for my protection. I couldn't believe he was more worried about the danger of my double lifestyle than the possibly of me betraying him. Reed really was a diamond in the rough.

"Come sit down, babe, and let me help make you calm," Reed begged, not for the first time since we arrived. Something about the whole thing; leaving our seconds in charge and having my cover blown just put me on edge. His body hadn't even offered much comfort; only a distraction.

This time, though, I listed and sat next to him, letting him put his arm around me. "You do realize you were my target when I got into town, Reed. I could have put you in jail. You're not pissed at me even a little?"

"Siren, you risked your job and your life for me from the moment you let me have that damn sexy body of yours. You're damn special, and I'm not letting you go so easily. Besides, you've always been on my side; you just didn't know it." I liked it when he teased, kissing down my neck. His dark facial hair tickled my skin.

I laid back on the bed, letting his lips explore my face and my collar bone, trying to lose myself in his touch. It was easier than I expected at a time of such stress between the two of us. I had been so sure the moment he found out about me, moments like this would just be taken away.

I sat up and shrugged off my jacket as Reed's hand slid under my shirt, grasping at my right breast. I moaned and laid back down, savoring the warmth of his expert touch as he massaged it. I let my foot slide up his left leg as he lay on the side of me with a sneaky grin. I could feel his bulge growing through his jeans, and I knew what he wanted.

"Isn't this nice?" I asked, beginning to relax a little. It was like Reed had magical powers over me. I wondered if every woman was this lucky to find a man that drove them crazy like this, or if it was just me. "We get to be alone for a change in a new city. Just the two of us." The last part came out breathy as his hand slipped down from my breast to my navel and began making circles just the way he might on that special spot. My panties were getting wetter by the moment.

"It's always nice to be in bed with you," he growled back softly, bending his head down to mine to nibble and lick at my earlobe. I closed my eyes and sighed, moving my ear into his mouth while his hand traveled down further to the button in my pants. He quickly did away with them, leaving my legs bare and my pink satin panties exposed. I purred and rocked my hips into him as he found my sweet spot, rubbing it just the way I liked.

I flipped over to my side and draped a leg over his back so that as I rocked my hips, they pressed directly into his body. Reed had his poker face on, but I knew it was driving him crazy.

He began to rub me harder, and then I gasped as he slipped a single finger inside my slippery center. My head went back in response. He had all the power over me at that moment, rubbing the inside of my pussy just the right way.

Then, he pushed my back down against the bed and slid my panties right off, making me watch as he slowly took off his jeans and boxers. I was ready to worship at the shrine of his manhood at that point, needing his body so badly to heal my shattered heart and mind.

Suddenly, he dragged me to the end of the bed, spreading my legs so he could wrap each one around him. My heart raced inside my chest at the anticipation as I felt the tip of his shaft knocking at the door to my pussy. Finally, he began to push inside of me, slowly. I hated that, and he knew that. But that was why he always did it.

My center dripped as he slid deeper inside of me, so turned on I could barely stand it. But Reed stood his ground and pumped into me in slow motion, barely hitting my G-spot before pulling back and starting the motion over again.

I used my feet to try and force him to fuck me faster, but he wouldn't budge; only smiled that deviant smile of his as he continued to tease me with his thick cock.

Finally, I could feel myself getting close when my cell began to buzz. No way was I answering it right now as I began to quiver and pulse with Reed inside of me. I knew who it was and how pissed they would be that I didn't answer, but I was coming from my boyfriend's shaft right now.

After he had unloaded into me as well, making me feel warm and satisfied, I shot up and picked it up immediately as it rang again. "He's ready for the both of you, but he's not happy about this, Elena. You need to tread lightly. Is there any chance you can leave the hot muscle man behind?" If I hadn't been so worked up, I would have laughed at Kristie's assessment of Reed.

"No, sorry." As soon as I said it, the line went dead. Kristie's wrath was bad enough to face. He had quite the temper, but she was also my best friend. I didn't risk a fall out with her over my crazy decisions on this case, but her boss, who I only knew by the generic name John, was another story. I had met him only twice; once on my second ever assignment for the bureau, and then again when I first became a handler for Richard's sake. Neither had been the most pleasant of meetings.

"Let's roll," I announced to Reed, and he immediately snapped into action, handing me a helmet. We hadn't seen any reason to cover up our identities in Cincinnati. It wasn't the ideal place for any kind of cartel or sex trafficking ring, and the

MCs were both back in Tennessee until I gave the Vipers a different order. It felt better to be more of myself now that I was back where I lived. It was like a test almost, to see if the freer me would still fit in with the cold city I'd run to after the horrors of Texas.

Our recent run-in with the men in blue had Reed driving more carefully, especially now that he knew what was at stake. So, it took quite some time in lunch rush traffic to get to the towering government building downtown where I would find Kristie and John on one of the top floors, guarded by three security checks.

It wasn't the hassle I expected, telling me they were just as worried about the situation as I was. It was no joke to be involved so deep with two shady organizations who were close to knowing who I was as an FBI agent. The first thing they did was immediately gave Reed security clearance, an honorary title on the project, and a long lecture about how serious the whole thing was. Reed seemed more amused by it than anything. I knew my man could handle anything, especially now that he knew everything. After Jimmy had spilled his guts, I had spilled mine, balling my eyes out for fear of losing Reed. But nothing had changed for us. He was a keeper, and I had no more qualms about accepting the cut.

John took his dear sweet time showing his face, but when he did, I felt myself shivering in my leather boots. He was an intimidating 6'3" and never had a smile on his face. He sat down at the desk without a word, and we were left in the closed office with only the four of us; myself, Kristie, John, and Reed.

"Well, it seems you have gotten yourself into quite the predicament this time, Agent Johnson. You're very lucky that your target turned out to be relatively innocent. Otherwise, you would have been stripped of your position and reprimanded, possibly thrown out of the country for your reckless behavior. And Kristie, I am disappointed in how you are handling this agent."

Kristie's leg was bouncing with anxiety, and I felt incredibly bad for how I had dragged her into my shit. But I stood my ground despite it all, knowing it was the bureau's job for John to be an asshole. "You know very well I am one of the best damn agents you have, John, so why don't we get past this lecture and put pen to paper so that that I can get you your bad guys."

"Fine. But consider yourself on notice, Agent Johnson." I met him eye to eye and could see in that that he was also intimidated by me. My behavior scared him, and even more so now that I had so much pull with two MCs. I could wreak havoc for him and everyone else in the bureau if I wanted. No way was he letting me walk out of there without meeting my demands now. "The terms are all laid out in this contract; both the Skulls Renegade MC and the Vipers MC remain under our immunity as long as you give us insider information regarding this sex trafficking cartel."

I read over the contract anyway, knowing how the twist of words could ruin my career and Reed's life. But there was nothing that I saw out of place. Myself, John, and Kristie all signed, and we were finally out of that stifling office.

"I guess we get to pack up and go back to Tennessee now," I said with exasperation as I climbed on the back of the bike.

"No way; not yet," Reed insisted with an obvious smirk in his voice. "I want you to put on your best damn clothes and take me to the best damn restaurant in town. I want to wine and dine my Ol' Lady in the city before we go back to Kyle and the Vipers and all the drama back there."

I smiled at the idea. We had already broken so many rules, so why not? "Alright, but I wanna swing by my place," I told him, giving him the directions. Part of me knew I could use some more clothes from there, but I also wanted Reed to see my real home.

***

I looked hot, and I knew it. I had on a sleek black dress with a daring split all the way up to my hip. I put on stiletto-heeled boots and redid my makeup to perfection. We were seated in a ritzy downtown restaurant; the kind that overlooks the city through all-around glass windows. It was the kind of place where a glass was as much as a bottle elsewhere. But it was amazingly romantic.

I was just leaning over to take a bit of some decadent chocolate cake off his spoon when I heard my name and a familiar voice. "Elena?"

I slowly lifted my head and found myself face-to-face with Richard, or Dick as I liked to call him. He was alone, and probably there for some lame work meeting in the VIP lounge. He looked as if he had aged a decade since I last saw him. It was the ultimate revenge as his eyes raked over me in that dress, clearly happy with another man already.

"Well, hello there, Dick. It's good to see you," I said sarcastically, causing Reed to shoot around and look at my ex.

"Who's this asshole?" Reed asked with a snicker. "Is this the fiancé you told me about?" I nodded, and Richard looked stunned.

"Who is he?" Richard asked, his brow starting to sweat at the intensity of the encounter. From an outside perspective, Reed was intimidating, and I probably looked more like the woman he met rather than the one he molded me into once he put a ring on it.

"This is Reed. My boyfriend." I kept it simple, watching the confusion come over him. Had he really thought I was just going to fade away and come crawling back pitiful and alone later? I had never had trouble landing a man, whether the purpose was for a good fuck or commitment. Though, Reed was a special catch.

"Oh, well, you look good," Richard told me awkwardly before walking away. I couldn't help but burst out laughing at the chance meeting and waving my middle finger behind his back. Now I was kind of glad we had stayed in Cincinnati for the night. Otherwise, I never would have gotten to experience that hilarious spectacle. Even in all the chaos that had happened over this assignment, I knew I was better off now than I had been with him.

"I love you, Reed," I told him flat out, not wanting to make such a big thing of saying it or not anymore.

"Same to you, Siren."

CHAPTER 10

Elena

"So, what did you want to talk about, boss?" Dmitri appeared in Reed's office, which I had on loan for the moment until there was a clear meeting space for the Vipers MC. I still hadn't officially dealt with the title, and I needed to get things on track with both MCs if I was going to start the process of getting info to take down a Mexican cartel. That shit was serious business. I also needed to make sure that illegal operations were ceased as much as possible. I didn't want to dabble in the same things as my father.

"We need to talk about the plan going forward. Obviously, Vipers have a territory already, and you guys probably need to get back. I know I am here most of the time because of Reed, but I would like us to share the two territories. Your idea to start up a trade of women just like these guys do, and that's exactly what I want to happen. I want these women to be given new lives and get out of that shit, Dmitri. I also need to know what kind if shit Jimmy was involved in so we can nip it in the bud."

Dmitri's face told it all for me. He looked pained. "You are the Prez now, Elena, but I have a tough time seeing you as anything other than that abused little girl sometimes. It's how I knew you'd set shit straight. But you're not going to like what I have to tell you."

"Go on," I urged him. I needed to hear every little gory detail.

Dmitri described some horrors that not even I quite expected. Apparently, illegal weapons trade wasn't enough for my father, even though they made a pretty penny from it. The man had dabbled in the drug trade, sex trafficking (much like what had been suspected of the Skulls), and even child pornography there at the end. Dmitri assured me that the operation had been shut down the moment I had popped a cap into Jimmy's knees. But hearing what Jimmy had done to women, selling them off to these various rings as well as using the young ones for the pleasure of perverts, I had more determination than ever to turn it around and get these women out of this.

I mulled it all over in my head, knowing that any MC still needed a way to make money, and sometimes it required dabbling in seedy dealings. I was going to have to make a few compromises to keep the MC afloat for the sake of the families as well as to get the money together to buy these women from the cartels.

"Alright, so as far as drugs, I want you to stick to pharmaceuticals and marijuana; nothing shadier than that. Try to keep it as legal as possible. There are places now where you can register to grow the shit and get paid for it. There's no reason an MC couldn't make bank off that. The point is to get the Vipers as legit as possible while still staying afloat."

Dmitri nodded. "That's all we want, Prez. I think I can make that happen, But what else?"

"Shoot down the gun trade as soon as the current stock is all sold. Then, we can think about going the legal way with that; a pawn shop or something that one of you can run in downtown. I know those make bank." I was nodding, getting the creative juices flowing. It was in my blood after all, whether I liked it or not.

"Child pornography is fucking disgusting, but I can't deny there's money in sex. If there is anyone in the MC savvy at all with directing and film, then you can consider doing some amateur porn films. On the condition that these people are completely willing to star in these films. Do not force anyone into it and make sure they get a cut of the royalties. Got me?" Dmitri nodded in agreement.

"The last thing I need from you is a good setup in Texas for when I'm there. Clean whatever place you're running there now the fuck up and make me an office that didn't belong to my damn father." Dmitri chuckled at that.

"Yes, ma'am."

He saluted me in jest and left the room, leaving me to contemplate whether I felt worthy of such a position or not. I didn't know if I was bad enough or good enough.

A knock came at the door, and I called the person in, only to find that it was Reed. "How'd it go, Siren? Did you show him who's boss?" he asked in a lusty growl pulling me out of my chair and into his arms. He had this way of turning me on in an instant, no matter the time of day or what was going on. I thought back on the first time I landed myself in Reed's bed and was bewildered by the place we were at now; in love with me wearing his cut.

Reed sucked my lip into his mouth and made me moan loudly. I knew the office was far from sound proof, but I just couldn't help myself. Things had been a little too business and not enough pleasure.

"You know," I began, twisting around so that it was him in front of the office chair. "I've always wanted to fuck someone in their office."

CHAPTER 11

Elena

I looked at the man sitting in my brand-new office with complete disgust, though I wasn't going to let it show on my face. Seamus had been sent down here to hot-as-hell Texas with me to meet Juan, our most obvious connection to the Mexican cartel I was supposed to be reporting on. Reed had contacted him for me to set up the deal so that Vipers MC could start purchasing women from him as well. I wanted to make sure we got something good out of our work with these filthy assholes. And filthy was no understatement.

The man in front of me, Juan Gonzales, oversaw procuring and transporting women within the cartel. He had been making the transactions with Reed for a couple of years now. It was the only reason he was even giving me a meeting, but he was a pure low life.

His accent was thick, and his clothes were covered in dirt as if he had been rolling around in it all day. My office would need to be fumigated due to the smell once he left the place, and he kept picking at his teeth; which were mostly covered in dirty, gold caps. When he did the picking, it made this awful smacking sound that made me want to lash out and slap him across the face. But I knew that wouldn't get me anywhere, even with Seamus by my side just in case.

"So, Reed says you want to start buying girls from me like he does. Is that right, *chica*?" As he said it in his thick Mexican accent, his eyes raked over me like I was a piece of meat, and it made me feel so dirty. I couldn't imagine what these women and girls he had in his possession were going through with him as their caretaker. He was a sick fuck.

"Yes. I would like to cut a similar deal with you if you're interested," I told him flatly. I was beginning to sweat, and I made a note to mention to Dmitri about getting some damn air conditioner in there. No way was I doing business in this hell hole without some cool air blowing my way. It was bad enough being back in Texas, to begin with. I hated the memories it brought back.

"That is if you have enough product to offer to us." I almost gagged at the thought of referring to human beings as objects for sale like that, but if I was going to deal with Juan, I would have to play the part. I could not risk him finding out what I was up to. It could out more than my own life in danger.

"I promise that we have plenty of beautiful women from all over the world to offer you, *chica*. Whatever you want, they will do for you. We know the best ways to break them." Juan sounded like a snake as the words slithered off his tongue like he was savoring them. I felt sick to my stomach. All I had to do was make the deal, and then I could throw up all I wanted. It was a mantra I kept going in my head as I stared him down with authority.

"Good. What terms do you propose? I want a good deal here, but I'm not going to go cheap on you if you offer me a good product." I raised my eyebrows at him for effect, gripping the arms on my seat.

"I am glad to hear it, and I am sure my boss will too. All we require is a trade at the border. We will disclose the location via phone message. I trust you have a phone that can't be easily traced?" I held up my burner phone and nodded. Little did they know the same phone that was making black market deals would also be informing the FBI about the goings-on with their cartel as soon as I was aware of it.

"Bueno. Then, you'll come with the cash and hand it over to me, and you'll get the agreed upon number of girls. You can inspect them if you want before you leave. It's that simple." Juan shrugged as if it was no big deal. How many of these contracts had he put together over the years? He looked to be in his late 30s or early 40s and had probably worked for the cartel a good half of those. I could only hope that between Reed and I we could save a large chunk of these women from going somewhere else where they would have no chance at a happy life.

"It does sound simple. I'm ready to make the deal, Juan, and to put in my order if you're ready for it." Juan nodded and stood up, reaching out his black hand to shake.

"What do you require, *chica*?" he asked with a savage hiss.

I thought long and hard about what they might have and how to make my selection the most impactful for the girls and for the FBI. "I want three girls with this first order. I want two of them to be young; as young as you've got. The other I want to be over the age of 25. Give me a mix of races and body types. I'm not picky about that. Is that something you can handle?"

"I already have the three women in mind, *chica*. I can get all three to you within a week. Show up at the location I give you with a flat $50,000." I shook his greasy hand again, and he pulled me in with a disgusting smile before Seamus escorted him out. A chill went down my spine, and I turned around to the trash can, spilling my guts immediately. Much like my father, Juan had been stripped of his humanity. There was no other way a human being could treat others quite so coldly.

CHAPTER 12

Elena

"Just pull off here," I ordered Dmitri. I had had him drive a large van out to the border where we to meet Juan and the women we were purchasing. I had wads of cash sitting in a backpack in the backseat, ready to hand over to Juan in trade for the three girls he would be handing over to me. I had not been given any details other than that they matched my exact specifications.

It was about an hour and a half before dawn as we pulled to the side of a dirt road outside of El Paso. The road had a large dip in it that would hide them inside of a shallow ditch as the trade was made. Not that there were many cars driving by apart from some sleepy truck drivers.

The large van would hold the three girls, myself, Dmitri, Seamus, and Jenna who had volunteered to come along and help me keep the girls calm. We had no idea what they were expecting and what trauma they had been through. We needed to be certain two women were available to make them feel as safe as possible. Hopefully, they would believe me when I told them we wanted to help them instead of abusing them.

A shiny, black SUV soon came down the hill and parked across from us. Its headlights were off, allowing it to blend into the dusty, early morning darkness. I nodded for Seamus to get out of the van with me just as I saw Juan and another man exit the SUV. I grabbed my bag of cash and dropped it at Juan's feet. "I'll think you'll find that the right amount is in there," I announced, nodding to the bag and keeping a couple of yards between us. I couldn't help but notice that the other man with Juan was easily half his age. Was life so bad for him that he ended up helping a Mexican cartel sell the bodies of young women at such a young age? That sort of business was full of victims, even if they weren't being raped every night.

"You are a friend of a good client. We want to show good faith here. No need to count the money, Miguel." Juan looked over at the younger man when he said this, revealing his name. It was another bit of information in my back pocket, though I hoped the young person would get off easy when everything was said and done. He didn't look like a fearsome killer and rapist to me; just a young man in an unpleasant situation.

"Let the record show that Vipers MC appreciates that," I nodded, glancing back at the vehicle. Surely the girls were scared and bound behind those tinted windows. It took all my willpower to stay still, waiting to get those women in my grasp and away from Juan.

"Miguel!" Juan barked at the boy, making him jump out of his skin. "Take the money to the car and get the girls. I'm sure that the Vipers are anxious to see what they have received." Miguel nodded and ran to the SUV, practically throwing in the back and reaching in to grab an arm and yank her out.

I could see that the woman was African American, curvy, and older, maybe 28 or 29. She had probably been a slave for the cartel for quite some time, cooking and cleaning for them. They trusted her enough that she had minimal bonds and nothing to cover her face. "This one is great for service. She had been broken by many of my amigos for the last several years. I hope she serves you just as well." Miguel walked the woman over and handed her to Seamus who held her tightly. She looked tired more than anything.

Miguel went back into the vehicle and pulled out the next woman. This one had a bag over her head, and her hands were tied with a rope. She was a good head shorter than the other woman and clearly younger. They had her dressed in a revealing skirt and top that allowed for her breasts to spill over. If I had to guess, this one was of Hispanic descent and under the legal drinking age or at least close to it.

"This one is a newer catch of ours from an enemy's home. She is very complaint but a little timid at first," Juan explained as this one was also handed off to Seamus.

I was getting impatient as Miguel finally went back for the last girl. As soon as Miguel reached in, I could hear her blood-curdling screams before she was slapped several times into submission. I tried my best not to cry or react when she was brought out as I realized what that the hefty sum of money had bought me.

The girl was young; too young, and bound at the feet and wrists. There was also a bag over her head. From the way her screams were now muffled; I could only guess that she probably had a gag as well. She was thin and pale with red hair spilling down her back. Worst of all, they had her dressed in lingerie that barely covered her body.

"Rafael handpicked this girl himself," Juan said with pride as the girl was handed over into my arms. She squirmed and tried to break free so that Seamus had to help me set her on the ground, and I held her arms tightly. I hated the fear and the torture I was putting this young girl through, but it was the only way to keep a hold of her for now. "She has not been trained, but she is beautiful. If she gives you trouble, we can always take her back."

"I like the feisty ones," I told him with a seductive growl, wanting to make sure I didn't let this one slip back into their filthy fingers. I knew more than ever that I was doing the right thing. I couldn't let young girls be treated this way. I knew I had my work cut out for me with this scared little girl, though.

"I see," Juan said, nodding as if he was picturing the whole scenario in his head with this girl and me. But the good news was that this encounter had given me two more names and three women that would never have to face predatory men like that again. I couldn't wait to reveal it to them. "When you or the Skulls are ready for the next shipment, you know where to find me. It was a pleasure." He winked at us before getting into his SUV and driving back onto the road. I waited until his taillights were far in the distance before I turned my back to the road and began helping Seamus load the girls into the van.

The red head in my arms was still fighting and screaming as Jenna helped me get her buckled into the middle between Jenna and the Hispanic woman. I sat in the middle row with the African American woman, as the men filled up the front.

"Are we ready to roll?" Dmitri asked as I finally got to buckle my seatbelt and slide the door shut. I nodded in confirmation, and we pulled out onto the road with the deafening screams of the young girl ringing in our ears. I waited until we were a good mile out before I tried to speak to them. I had hoped calmness would come over them, but the screams had just turned into desperate tears.

"I need you all to listen to me!" I yelled with authority. I hated to be harsh, but it was all they were going to respond to right now. "I need you to shut your fuckin' mouth so I can tell you what's going to happen when I take you home with me."

The women were quiet; the African American woman was training her tired eyes on me. "What does a woman want with us, anyway?" she dared to ask. "Are you a lesbian or something?"

I shot her a look, so she knew I meant business. I wasn't going to beat the shit out of her like those men probably had, but I wasn't going to let anyone's attitude get in the way of accomplishing this. "No, I am not a fuckin' lesbian. Now, I don't expect you to believe me with whatever it is you've been through, but I am not going to hurt you or make you my slave. I'm not going to let anyone do that to you anymore if you listen and let me help you. I'm going to have my friend, Jenna here, remove the sheets off your heads, but I need to know you won't fight or scream. Can you promise me that?"

The Hispanic woman was the first to nod, and Jenna reached over and lifted her sheet off. I was hoping that the young one would allow us to do it too, but she shook her head and continued crying.

I turned around in my seat as Jenna began to coax the woman into talking. She apparently had been crying silent tears for a while, the stains from them streaked across her tan face. "How old are you, sweetheart?" Jenna asked calmly. "How did you end up here?"

The woman glanced back and forth between Jenna and I a few times before opening her mouth. "I'm 19." I took a deep breath, knowing that I should have expected this when I asked for someone young. "My father makes drugs for Senor Rafael, and he didn't deliver enough a couple of months back. So, I was taken as payment. Along with my sister. She was taken for Senor Rafael himself."

I shook my head at the idea of a father getting into drug trade when he had a daughter at home. She was probably used to harsh conditions at this point. "How old was your sister?" I dared to ask. I probably didn't want to hear it.

"She is 17, Miss. I haven't seen her in two months." I looked at her with sympathy, and Jenna picked up her hand and patted it.

"What about you, hun, what's your story?" I asked, looking at the older woman who sat beside me.

"I'm about to be 30, I think. It's easy to lose track of your birthday. They found my one night about six or seven years ago coming out of a strip club and took me. I've been their slave for a very long time now. They haven't treated me too badly in the last few years because they trust me, and I'm too old to be in any of those men's beds." I nodded, listening to her. If they trusted her so much, she might have heard things. She could easily come in handy later.

I looked at the young girl who has since quit sobbing. I nodded to Jenna to take off her sheet and remove her gag while I worked at the ties on the other girls' hands. I didn't think they would run now. They both seemed to be calm.

I tried not to focus on the red and swollen face of the young teenager in the back seat. She had cute little freckles all over her face and long orange-red hair. "It's okay baby. You can tell us what happened," Jenna coaxed, pulling the shivering girl into her arms. I could see bruises on her body both fresh and old and could tell she was deathly afraid.

"We want to help you. We won't let those bad men get to you again, okay?" The girl nodded and rocked back in forth in Jenna's arms as her hoarse voice began to explain where she came from. It instantly broke my heart. This girl was not the kind to normally be at any risk for such a horrible thing to happen. She had a family out there somewhere looking for her.

"My name is Kimberley," she told us. "I just turned 15." She squeaked that part out as tears began to stream down her face again. I couldn't fuckin' wait for the day that Rafael and Juan were going to be locked away for good and tried for their horrible crimes. They were going to rot in there. "My family and I were having a vacation in Cabo when they took me. It was horrible. Are you guys serious about helping me? I really want to find my parents and my little brother." Jenna pulled Kimberley into her chest and cradled her like she was her own child.

"We'll do everything we can," I told her confidently. "I'm sure your family must be out there looking for you, which means they'll be loud and easy to find. For now, we're going to get you all some clothes and get your birth certificates and everything you need before we talk about the next step. If you're up for it, you'll have the chance to join an MC and earn some cash and have a place to live. We can also try and get you set up with a real job if you'd like."

The women looked hopeful despite their scars and the obvious beatings they'd taken. I felt like all my hard work on this crazy case was not going to be in vain.

***

I sat down at the bar, feeling the exhaustion taking over me as I ordered a drink from Daisy. The older woman, I had left in Dmitri's hands. She had been ready and willing to join the ranks of the Vipers immediately. She was going to be a strong asset, I could already tell. The two younger girls opted to come back to Tennessee with me and were sharing a room with Jenna, whom they had bonded with on the way over. It was a side of Jenna I hadn't seen before, but apparently, she had a real motherly instinct in her. She had been able to make both the girls comfortable and sang them to sleep.

"You know, I just really admire what'ch'yer doin' with these girls," Daisy leaned over the counter and told me with a warm smile. She seemed to be more of herself than the last time we had spoken, so I hoped that meant Kyle had straightened his shit out as she told him to. "It's amazing to see them escape and turn into beautiful young women."

"I agree with that," Seamus said, suddenly lifting his drink in a toast. Michelle and I both noticed the fact that he was making clear goo-goo eyes at Daisy and started to snicker.

"Seamus, I can smell your BS from here!" Michelle belted out with a laugh. "You have a crush on Daisy." Seamus put his head down and walked away with several of the women heckling him along the way. I caught a slight blush in Daisy's cheeks as she turned around and went back to work, wiping down the bar and getting everyone else their drink orders. What was that all about?

I didn't have much time to think about it as I felt warm arms embrace me from behind. I turned around in my seat to see Reed, my number one man standing there with a smile on his face. The first thing he did was give me a kiss that would have made me fall to my knees had I been standing. It had only been a few days that we had spent apart, but it felt like a century. Who knew a bad ass FBI chick like me would fall so hard for a man again so soon after being played by my asshole fiancé? It felt like I had won a contest to get Reed, though.

"I'm so proud of you, babe,' he whispered in my ear before ordering a round of drinks for everyone. "I want you all to raise your fuckin' glasses for my bad ass Ol' Lady here!" he called out, raising his beer high in the air so that it splashed out a little onto his hand and jacket.

Everyone raised their glasses and cheered before downing their drinks. Then, Reed hauled me over his shoulder and took me into the bedroom, throwing me down and locking the door behind us.

-

CHAPTER 13

Reed

I slowly got dressed, being as quiet as possible not to wake Elena. I wanted to be able to come back to her when I was through seeing what the hell was going on so damn early in the morning in my bar. I could hear breaking glass and screaming through the closed door and quickly headed in that direction.

I should have fuckin' known who was responsible for the racket as I approached Daisy's bedroom door. The only person who could get her that pissed off was my asshole, evil twin brother, Kyle. He had been in and out of the bar for a while now, and I still had no fuckin' clue what he was around for. The guy straight up abandoned his post as Prez of Skulls Renegade MC and dumped the shit in my lap to fix after my father retired. He had been grooming Kyle to take over for years until he was done and just left, leaving us a fuckin' note. Haven't even seen the Ol' Man in years.

I loved to ride my motorcycle and look like a badass for the ladies. Hell, I had even gotten into a fight or two where I beat the shit out of a few deserving assholes, but I had never been for this lifestyle of fucking people over for money and getting into illegal shit. The moment I got my hands on the operation, we went legit and never looked back. I made these people my family and was damn sure that Kyle would never walk back into mine or Daisy's life.

I wanted to kill him when Daisy finally made it back to us and told me what happened. I was one of the only ones who knew just what the two of them went through. She hadn't even revealed everything to Elena yet, who was clearly her best friend in the house.

I remembered the state Daisy came back in; bloodied and bruised with a warning to never cross the damn loan shark my stupid brother got involved with again. I was lucky to be able to redo the bar and pick this shithole back up off its feet and get the MC running again. It came as second nature now.

I banged on the door with my fist. "You better fuckin' open up and quit the racket before you wake up my Ol' Lady. She's not a morning person!" I warned, which was the truth. If she found out Kyle and Daisy were goin' at it again, she'd probably knock him out despite him being twice her size. She didn't let anyone mess with the people she loved, which was one of my favorite things about that Siren of mine.

Kyle burst through the door, looking furious; his face all red like a fire. Did I look like that when I got mad? "What the fuck is going on here, Kyle? I told you if you were going to be here I didn't want any fuckin' trouble going on. You were to lay low and fix shit with Daisy, and here you guys go waking me up at the rack of fuckin' dawn with your yelling and throwing shit."

I pushed him back into the bedroom and shut the door. I wanted this solved once and for all. Daisy looked like she had been crying and exerting herself letting me know she was the one throwing this around. At least I wouldn't have to take my own brother out for being violent with a lady. "One of you better start fuckin' talking before I beat it out of you," I threatened I didn't want any of this nonsense going on at my club, especially with the FBI watching us. Not that anyone but Elena and I knew that. But it was a big deal. She could trust a piece of paper all day long, but I sure as hell didn't. I knew we were walking a thin line with the law here.

"I'm trying to do what Irish told me to do and settle things with Daisy here. I know I have shit to make up for, and I know I'm an ass whose hard to swallow. But this damn woman won't even hear me out at all. I can't make up with something like that. So, what am I supposed to fuckin' do? Disappear again?" I sighed and put my head in my hands. I didn't know how to handle this shit. I wasn't a mediator; just a Prez of an MC. I could talk business and fight all day, but not this emotional stuff. I didn't have these problems with Siren. She was my everything, and I wasn't about to disappoint her. So, how was I to see where my brother was coming from.

"She didn't tell you to come in here and get back with me, you pig!" Daisy yelled at him with her arms crossed over her chest. "You wanna apologize, you wanna make it up to me? Well, you sure as hell can try, but I doubt it's going to work. But I am not some damsel who's going to fall back into your arms just because you burst through those doors again after leaving us all high and dry. I'm too damn strong for that."

"Can the two of you give me just five minutes?" I asked, and they nodded. The only way this was going to get solved is by putting my head together with someone who had a higher emotional intelligence than myself, especially when it came to women.

"Siren," I whispered, leaning down to her ear and kissing her forehead a few times. "I know it's early, but Daisy and Kyle need our help." I watched as the goddess that had somehow become my Ol' Lady stretched her naked body out on my bed and smiled up at me. It didn't matter if she had bed head or someone's blood on her or if she was wearing the most expensive damn lingerie money could buy, she was the sexiest woman I had ever been allowed to lay my hands on. I felt damn lucky every time she let me look in those eyes of hers and touch the most intimate parts of her.

"Can't we just go back to bed?" she teased with her signature pout. I always got mad at her for that because it killed me and made my dick wiggle to life every fuckin' time. She knew just how to drive me nuts.

"No, I'm sorry, babe. It's bad this time." She sat up with concern and went into action, slipping on jeans and a tee-shirt before brushing her beautiful long hair that made her look so much like a siren rather than an average human woman.

"I'll take Kyle into my office, alright? I think you and Daisy have some things to talk about, and then maybe we can come up with a solution for this. They woke me up with their fight this morning."

Elena nodded, look determined as we went back to Daisy's room.

"Morning, Irish." Kyle apparently couldn't help himself, and one of these days it was going to get him shot. Elena gracefully ignored it, though, and went to sit on the bed next to Daisy as I pulled my brother into my office. I needed to get to the bottom of this.

"Kyle, I don't wanna play games anymore. Daisy is an important part of the Skulls, and I can't have you messing with her head all the time. It's time, to be honest about why you're here." I laid it to him straight. I didn't have the patience for it anymore.

"I came back for two reasons, brother. The first was to check on the responsibility that I just dropped on you. I wanted to make sure no one was suffering because of that decision. Regardless of how I left or why I did care about some of the people here." I tried to take what he said in stride without automatically reacting in frustration. It was hard to believe that he cared for people he just walked out on like that.

"What's the second reason?" I asked him, point blank.

"I came to get Daisy back."

***

Elena

"Dais, what's going on with Kyle? I asked him to fix things with you so he could stay here, but I'm worried about the both you at this point. Reed and I both are," I said softly, placing my hand on her shoulder.

"Oh, Elena, I was so sure all of it was in the past, and I would never have to talk about it again. But here he is, showing his sorry face around here like he's gonna win me back. It's makes all those memories come back to me. I just wanna punch him for thinkin' it's that simple. I don't think my heart can be won back after everything that went down here."

I shook my head and gave her a quick embrace. "Dais, it must be hard to talk about, but maybe if you tell me what happened, other than him leaving, then I could help you out here. You know I've been through some tough shit too. I mean, I just shot my father dead less than three weeks ago. You can tell me anything."

"Oh, I believe you, Elena. If Reed trusts you, I trust you. It's just hard to talk about when I've tried to put it in the past. You see, things were bad once Kyle took over. He and his old man got into a lot of arguments over how to handle the MC, and we were hemorrhaging money like crazy. Once his old man left, all we had left was Kyle. Reed wasn't around. He wasn't that interested in this kinda life. So, Kyle was runnin' us into the ground. I tried to keep him sane. I loved that man so, but he got in with a nasty loan shark he couldn't pay back. The best way the loan shark saw fit to get back at him was to take someone he loved…"

Daisy trailed off and put her head in her hands. It was the second time I had seen her cry since I'd met her. This tough chick really had been through hell and back. I could only imagine how closely her tale, after that point, matched up with some of the things the girls I had just brought home with me, had been through. Loan sharks were nasty business. You didn't fuck with 'em unless you could walk the walk, and Kyle didn't strike me as the type who could.

"They took you, didn't they?" I asked her, rubbing her back as a mother might. Kyle really left her to that?

Daisy nodded. "Yeah, and they did things to me," she admitted. She didn't need to clarify. "They had me for a good month before Reed came for me with the news that Kyle had just up and fuckin left me and the MC. So, he got me kidnapped and tortured and just ran off, leaving me for dead. They only let me go because Reed promised them the money and because Kyle clearly didn't care about me enough anymore to make it worth it for them."

By the end of her story, I was fuming. I don't know how in the world I was ever going to be able to look Kyle in the eyes again. I had known he was a self-righteous ass, but this was more than that. "I want you to take the day off. I'll see if Michelle can handle the bar for you today, okay? You go and pamper yourself, and we'll deal with Kyle."

Daisy nodded and went to get dressed while I went to see what that heart-to-heart looked like between Reed and Kyle because I was damn well expecting it to turn into a fist-to-fist situation. But when I knocked on the door of Reed's office and walked in, I found a very different scene from what I thought I would. Kyle had the hint of tears in his eyes and instantly stormed out when I came into the room. "What the hell?" I asked, pointing in the direction he went. Reed patted his lap, and I sat on it. He gave me a sweet peck on the cheek.

"I really hate to say this, but I think my brother has better intentions of begin here than I thought. Though, he did make mention of a few pieces of business we're doing that he doesn't like. I made sure to give him the what for on that," Reed told me, pretending to look tough. It made me laugh.

"Reed, you know what happened to Daisy because of him, right?" I asked softly, running my fingers against his scratchy facial hair.

"So, she told you then?" I nodded. "I knew she would at some point. I'm one of the only people here who knows. She was in an awful state; I know that. But he's explained some things to me, and you're just going to have to trust me on this one for now."

"Just please don't let him keep coming around here and making her hurt," I begged.

"We came to an understanding. He's gonna be around but only as a legitimate member, under my direction, and he is to leave Daisy alone unless she approaches him first. I got this." I smiled and kissed his cheek.

"My man always has things handled."

CHAPTER 14

Elena

"Hello, is this Miriam Lauten?" I asked into the receiver. I had made it my mission for the past few days to figure out where Kimberley's family was. She had told me she was from Denver, and so that's where I had started my research. There had to be a family out there searching for their missing daughter and a missing person's case to go along with it in both Cabo and Denver. I had been right about that, and once I had identified myself, the officers on the case were thrilled to give me the name and number of her mother and let me take it from there.

"Yes, this is she," the woman said. Her tone was polite, but I could hear her exhaustion and sadness clear as day. The woman was trying to care for a first grader while her teenage daughter was missing, and she had no answers and no hope. I was so happy to be able to give her great news. "May I ask who is speaking?"

"My name is Elena, and I'd like you to hear me out because I have a crazy story to tell you about your daughter, Kimberley."

"Kimberley! You know where Kimberley is?" The woman sounded like she might faint from shock. I could hear her calling her family members to the phone in the background. "We're all here, listening. Please, tell us if our sweet Kimberley is okay," she begged through tears.

"I'm not going to lie, Kimberley has had a rough time of it, but we were able to actually buy her from one of the men that took her in Mexico. She's in Tennessee right now with us. We've been feeding her and getting her some clothes. She's really shaken, but she's alive and asking me to find you guys. So, I'm glad I was able to do that for her. Is there any way that one of you can come and get her? I don't think she should be sent on a plane or bus alone right now." Kimberley was going to need a lot of help. She cried herself to sleep at night and often woke up with blood-curdling screams from horrible nightmares, but she was healthier and happier knowing that she was safe. I hoped that seeing her family would put another spark back into her that I could barely see a hint of right now.

As I revealed the news to her family, I could hear all arrays of reactions; cheering, clapping, howling with tears of joy…I was so happy that at least one of these girls was going to have a real family to go back to. I was beginning to understand why Reed was so forgiving with Kyle. Not a whole lot of people on Earth could replace your actual family.

Miriam was obviously overwhelmed, and a male picked up the phone. "This is Kimberley's father. We're going to try and catch a flight tonight.

Thank you so much for getting our Kimberley back."

As soon as I got off the phone, I went straight for Jenna's room and knocked on the door. I found Kimberley on her belly in the bed, reading a book Jenna had bought for her about overcoming abuse. She didn't smile when I came into the room, but she did sit up and acknowledge my presence. It had been hard to explain to her that they were a motorcycle club that bought her from the cartel and yet they were good people. She only trusted Jenna, and just really didn't understand their motive. I guessed that she had lost her faith in most people during the abuse she suffered at the hands of Juan and his cohorts.

"I have some good news for you," I told her with a smile. I was careful not to touch her because she was still very sensitive about that.

"You found my parents?" she asked, cocking her head to the side.

"I did. And I just got off the phone with them. Your mother and father will be on a plane tonight to come and get you. They sounded so happy." Kimberley reached out and hugged Jenna with a happy squeal and then she hugged me.

"Thank you for saving me."

***

The bar was pumping with loud, lively music, and everyone was in party mode. Kimberley's parents picked her up, things were going well with the Vipers MC, and things were beginning to run smoothly. I had gotten a report that Dmitri had gotten a small group together to make a film and that one of the members was able to get a grower's silence for weed in Colorado. He would run it out of a house the MC bought for him along with a couple of other members. Things felt so good; I almost forgot I was on an assignment and not just living life.

I went up to Daisy with a smile on my face. She had come back from a spa day looking beautiful and refreshed, and I could see that Kyle was keeping his distance. She and Michelle were taking it upon themselves to take Maria, the 19-year-old we'd bought from the cartel, under their wings and teach her how to cook and serve. She was doing a pretty decent job, and it gave me an idea.

"You know, Daisy, this is a real nice bar," I told her. "But don't you think it could be even better?"

"Oh no, Elena, I know that look. You've got some idea in that big brain of yours. Where do they all come from anyway?" she teased, sounding more like her playful self. "So, what did ya have in mind?"

I tapped my nails against the counter thoughtfully. I had idly been thinking on it for a while. The women that decided to stay with us after we rescued them would need an occupation of some kind. It would be best for them to earn their keep and have something to occupy their mind after all the trauma they had been through. Seeing how well Maria was doing as a server just made me think the answer was in the bar, right in front of me. "Well, let's face it, these women will need somewhere to work. What if we just expanded the bar a little more? We could have a real dance floor and a mechanical bull. We could serve some real food, maybe even a full menu some nights like sports bars do. I mean, it's a small town. People could use a more fun place to come to after work."

I felt a pair of hands go around my waist and knew that Reed was behind me. He leaned down and gave me a scrumptious kiss on my neck that made me feel like I was melting inside. "What's going on over here, ladies?" he asked.

"You better watch out, Reed. Your Ol' Lady is talking about doin' stuff to your bar," Daisy told him with a teasing smile.

Reed spun me around in his arms to face him. "What's this about?" he asked in amusement as he slid his hands up and down my lower thighs. He was driving me wild right there in front of everybody. It was pure torture; his specialty.

"I thought it would be a good idea to make this more like a real sports bar and restaurant. Give the girls a place to work when we bring them here and make a bigger impact on the community here." I tried to keep my cool as his hands traveled higher up. I could feel the warmth growing in both my cheeks and my groin.

"I think this is something better talked about in private," he said with his eyebrows raised.

I went with him like a loyal puppy dog as he dragged me up to the bedroom that was over the bar. There were whoops and clapping from some of the rest of the MC members. They knew the private conversation we were about to have would involve few words.

Reed led me back into the bedroom and slammed the door shut, locking it before turning on me with a glint in his eye. "I'm so hungry for you right now," he growled at me, looking like a lion coming for a gazelle. But it just served to excite me, and I was going to meet him right there.

I stripped down to nothing in fifteen seconds flat, raising my eyebrow at him. I loved being feisty with Reed. "Do I look appetizing to you?" I asked, turning in circles before strutting up to him and licking his lips seductively. A groan came from the back of his throat like an animal, but I took control this time before he had the chance; taking off his clothes just as quickly as I had mine. This time, things were going to go my way.

I pressed my body up against his, pulling his lip into my mouth with a sucking motion. He moaned into my mouth before I backed him onto the bed, straddling his body with mine. Reed's hands slid up my skin, giving me the best bout of goosebumps I'd ever had.

I lowered myself onto his rock-hard shaft, taking things slow only long enough to get my body settled. It was nice to be in control for a change and do things the way I wanted them to be.

"Mmmm," I moaned at the feel of his cock moving inside me as I began to rock my hips back and forth. He reached around and grabbed the tops of my ass cheeks, squeezing them between his rough fingers. I squealed at the sudden sensation before bouncing up and down on his cock a little harder, letting my hair swing behind me and my ass slap down onto his hips.

I began to moan as his cock slipped deeper inside of me, pleasurably impaling my body. I grabbed his hands and put them on my hips, letting him rock me to completion like I was nothing but a rag doll until we both reached completion together.

With a happy sigh, I slid off him and rolled to his side, placing my head on his chest. My heart was still beating fast, and my breathing was labored as he began to play with my long, red locks.

"So, what was this proposal you had at the bar?" he asked, and I could feel the grin he had across his face. I poked him in his side, biting away a smile before explaining to him what I was thinking. "I think it sounds perfect, Siren."

Chapter 15

Elena

Reed was out dealing with club business, so I locked the bedroom door and decided it was high time to start giving the FBI what they wanted. We had gotten three girls from Juan, and all three were doing better than I had even imagined. Kimberley had been able to go home with her parents and was in counseling. Her parents called me occasionally to keep me updated as a thank you. I appreciated it since this little sweetheart had the same name as my mother. It made things feel like they were coming full circle.

The other two women had become involved with the MCs and were thriving in their new positions. It was a small victory, and I hoped before this all came crashing down we would be able to get some more. I had already asked Reed to set himself up for another meeting with Juan and ask for five girls this time. I wanted to get as many as possible out of this terrible life that I could.

"Hello?" Kristie's voice came through the line. I hadn't heard her voice in a while now, and I was glad it sounded happier than the last time we had spoken. Technically, I should have turned the information I had right over to John, but I didn't like dealing with him. He gave me the creeps. Besides, Kristie was still my handler and my best friend.

"Hey, Kristie," I said cheerily, wishing there was time to gossip right now, but I knew this was about business. "How are things going up there in Cincinnati?"

"Mostly, everyone's a nervous wreck waiting for you to give up any information. The bureau is whispering about you going rogue. Please, tell me you have something for me."

I scoffed. The bureau was always going to talk about me like that, but I had nothing to worry about unless I failed to give them the information they needed. So far, I had never failed an assignment despite my unconventional methods of getting the job done. "I do have something for you. We purchased three girls, and these girls gave us quite a bit of information. I am not sure yet if it will be enough to do anything. One of the women may be cooperative. She's joined the Vipers, and she'd been with the cartel quite a while." I was still sure she would be our smoking gun, especially now that she was loyal to me as the Prez of the Vipers. I knew she had to know something of use.

"Well, that's better than I expected. I will let the bureau know to go pick her up at the Vipers headquarters in Texas so they can talk. I'll make sure she knows she's totally safe, and I won't let them blow your cover. I'll just say because

Kimberley was a minor, we are investigating the whole incident." I agreed, knowing Kristie and her team would know just how to handle this. I wasn't really worried about that. But this sleazy cartel was really bugging the shit out of me, and I knew they had the power to take me down if they knew what I was doing.

"Just keep things quiet. I don't need the cartel getting wind of this."

"I agree," Kristie said, and I could hear her typing in the background. "That's exactly why I don't think you should give up any info over the phone, even on this phone. You need to come back to the office and give John and I all you know. And please, don't bring your boyfriend this time. That created quite a frenzy. Plus, it'll look funny if both of you suddenly disappear again. We want to keep all of you own there as safe as we can." I didn't like what she was suggesting, and Reed wouldn't either, but I also knew Kristie was right. I was getting into dangerous territory, and I needed to be more careful.

"He's not going to like it, but I get it. When do you want me there?" I asked, already knowing the answer. It was probably going to be soon because the bureau just loved their open and shut cases. The longer something took to solve, the more nervous and demanding they got. It was a bureaucratic annoyance, but it was part of the job. So, I had to go with their flow.

"As soon as you could get here would be great. Just don't be suspicious about it, and make sure there's always someone protecting your people, Elena. This is serious." Kristie was talking as my friend now rather than my handler. She must have realized how much this assignment had turned into real life for me and how much I cared about these MC members. I hadn't even thought about what I would do once I was released from this assignment. I couldn't help but tear up just a bit at the thought.

"I'll make some arrangements and leave as soon as I can. I want to be here for the next shipment of girls if I can, so I'll need to check with Reed."

"Alright, Elena. I'll see you soon."

I hung up the phone and laid back on the bed just listening to myself breathing. It hadn't ceased to amaze me over the last several weeks and months since arriving in Tennessee how much of a 360 my life had done. I was still left dizzy from the change. I was on the marriage track before with a corporate, buttoned-up man who had apparently been using long hours at work as an excuse to cheat on me. My career was boring me, and I kept my wild side under wraps for the potential of a new life on the mommy track with a nice picket fence. Now, I was the Ol' Lady to a damn hot MC Prez and was an MC Prez myself. My lousy ass father was long gone from this Earth, and revenge was mine. I was back undercover, and it felt like me all over again; someone I could look at in the mirror and recognize.

I must have dozed off like that because I woke up to a knock on my door. I went to it and unlocked it, finding Reed standing there, looking amused. "For a minute there, I was afraid you had another man in there," He teased, looking around as if he might find someone hiding in the closet. I slapped his shoulder playfully.

"No other man would put up with me," I told him, pulling him down onto the bed with me in a flurry of giggles. "Besides, no other man can turn me on like you do." He grabbed a chunk of my ass and squeezed. I liked how we were light and fun, but I knew I had to tell him about the call with Kriste.

"So, I ordered another five women," he told me, and I kissed him five times for that. "Does that make you happy?"

"It does," I told him, but then I gave a faux pout. "But what doesn't make me happy is what I have to tell you. I talked to Kriste, and she and John need me to come to Cincinnati to give them the info. They're afraid of me giving things away over the phone. They want me to get both MCs protected, and they're going to take Cecil for questioning. They don't want you to come with me. I think I have to follow the orders this time."

"You've gotta do what you've gotta do, Siren. I love ya either way. I just don't like the way they're always putting you in danger. But I've got the MCs covered, and I can handle picking up the women if that happens while you're gone. You don't worry about a damn thing." I felt a slight comfort at his acceptance of the situation, but I still had this nervous feeling I couldn't explain. Call it intuition, but something wasn't right.

***

I looked around my place with a smile on my face. I had to admit that as much as I missed Reed and Daisy, I loved being allowed to be back home for a little bit. Tennessee had its beauties, such as getting to see the mountains every day, but Cincinnati had better weather for me. I loved the cold; the complete contrast of the southern city I grew up in. Maybe one day we could move the headquarters for the Vipers and the Skulls Renegade up here. It was probably wishful thinking, but a girl could dream, right?

My phone began to buzz, and I picked it up, knowing what it must mean. It was around lunch time, and Kristie had finally sent the text I had been waiting on.

We're ready for you

I stood up and took my time, walking through every room and looking around. I doubted I would be sticking around to come back here again after I told them what I knew.

I went out to my rental car and climbed in, having opted for typical transportation and a more appropriate outfit this time. I hadn't totally ditched the leather, but I left my cut in the car and opted for some flats instead of my boots. I didn't think John had been too thrilled with my bad ass biker chick get up the last time I had been here.

I pulled up to the office and walked in, feeling a bit of deja vu as I headed up to a familiar room. I was quickly escorted into the office where John and Kristie were waiting.

Kristie stood up to give me a hug, happy to see me. It looked like John wasn't giving her any more shit since I had shown up to make good on my promise to give up what I knew.

"Alright, so start with what you know about the girls, and then you can go from there. Any names and details of these people would be great. A sketch of the vehicle. Anything at this point could lead us to crack down on this cartel." John was matter-of-fact and cold in his speech as always, but I gave him a dazzling smile anyway. I loved being   a smart ass.

Then, I began to relay all I knew; the story of the three women we had picked up, including the minor and where she had been kidnapped. I let them know Juan's name as well as Rafael's, who was their apparent leader. John seemed to be particularly interested in the two other women since one had a family with business dealings with the cartel and the other might have direct inside information that they could use.

"So, what do you think? Is this going to be enough to go on?" I asked, looking over the notes he had made on my statement.

"Technically speaking, it's not a ton to go on, but it's a good start. These two women might be a good find, and then the fact that they kidnapped and sexually assaulted a minor is a big one. It might be easier to get Mexico to extradite at this point or at least cooperate on charges and prison security."

I nodded along, hoping he was done being frustrated with Kristie and me.

Then, Kristie's phone rang, and she looked down at it with a strange expression. "For some reason, your boyfriend is calling me,' she said before answering it. Why would Reed call Kristie's phone and not mine? I only gave that to him in the case of an emergency. That had to mean something had gone wrong.

I sat on the edge of my seat as I watched Kristie's face droop with concern. "Alright, we'll do all we can to keep her safe. We'll see you soon." Kristie hung up and looked up at me with a pale face.

"Your cover's been compromised with the cartel. Reed's coming to meet you. You're going to have to go into hiding."

CHAPTER 16

Reed

I kept looking around nervously as we approached the border between Texas and Mexico near Laredo. It was only Seamus and me who had taken the van down to pick up the five girls we would be taking home this time. I also strapped my bike to a trailer on the back just in case. For some reason, even though I made a trade like this many times since becoming Prez of Skulls Renegade MC, I had this bad feeling in my gut. Seamus kept telling me it was because my Ol' Lady wasn't with me, but there was something more to it than that. It just didn't feel like every other time.

Juan had never gotten the girls to me this fast after an order, and he seemed desperate to get these girls off his hands. His tone on the phone had even been different than before. I knew I had told Elena that I could handle this by myself while she headed up to Cincinnati to take care of business with the FBI, but I was regretting accepting the meeting now.

Like always, I was given a specific road to pull off. This one led me into an abandoned neighborhood that looked like it used to be a booming industrial district, Now, it looked like one of those ghost towns you saw on the news occasionally. It was a pretty creepy setup with warehouses and dirt blowing all around. There was even a gas station that hadn't been visited in so long that the sign showed a gallon of gas as being under a dollar.

The place was dead quiet even though it was the middle of the day, and I hadn't even seen a cop in sight. Maybe it was the ideal halfway point if someone was coming in from Mexico illegally. I suspected I might see a starving and squatting Hispanic family or two if I hung around long enough. But I wasn't planning on being there any longer than I had to be. I was good at putting on a poker face, even with the worst of men, but the more women we got from Rafael and Juan, the more it made them seem like the lowest scum of the Earth. And it was hard to hold back the urge to squash them.

"Now, I'm feeling uneasy, boss," Seamus commented, as he pulled into an old covered parking spot under a jagged piece of metal. We were at the back of an old warehouse that looked like it was once painted white but was now covered in brown dirt. The dust clouds were blowing in my face as I exited the van.

I felt for the Glock hidden in my pocket, and I peeked over to make sure Seamus had his too. This place was fuckin' eerie, and I was going to be certain if I made it outta here alive I wouldn't be meeting with Juan to grab the girls here again.

I walked in the dark and abandoned place, mostly open and empty besides a few abandoned boxes and packing supplies. There was still one conveyor belt shoved into the corner. Other than that, my only company was Seamus, dirt, and the shit eating monster that was waiting for me at the other end of the large, haunting room.

He was alone, which worried me even more. I knew something wasn't right. I nodded to Seamus to give him a signal, and I saw that he tensed up around his own pocket, ready to strike if need be.

"Where are the girls?" I barked as I approached Juan with his rotting smile. He looked like a smug supervillain.

"Calm down, gentlemen. They are all in the car on the other side of the building. All five that you asked for are there. I thought that your associate here could go and load them out while the two of us had a little chat, man to man." I narrowed my gaze at him, having no idea what shit he was playing at, wanting to talk and to separate us, but because he was alone, I decided to make the priority the girls.

"Seamus, why don't you go see what this guy is talking about and see if you can't get these girls into the van without a fuss. Can you handle that?" Seamus nodded, and let go of the tough grip on his gun after passing an upset glance between the two of us. I could tell he didn't want me to be alone in there with Juan with the mood he seemed to be in, but we didn't really have an option. I had to play this game well, whatever it was, to make sure all seven of us were going to make it back to the bar safe and sound.

"So, what's this all about?" I asked, nodding towards Juan. I wasn't in the mood to wait for him to get through a roundabout explanation. I didn't take a fight stance, but I let him know he owed me an explanation.

"I came in here alone for a reason, Reed. It's because I respect you, and I trust you. We have been business partners for a long time, haven't we?" I nodded, not liking the way he was still insisting on going around in circles. "You see, I want to give you the benefit of the doubt here because I believe you to be totally innocent as far as in or business dealings. It doesn't matter to me what you do to or for these women once you have them, as long as you give me the money I ask for and keep your mouth shut about what we do here."

That feeling in my stomach was back as he began to pace with great bravado. He may have looked like a filthy shithead that was just some poor peon, but I knew him well enough to know Juan was nothing of the sort. He was a ruthless middle manager in a cartel who had a sadistic need to boss around all these young women. He had no respect, mercy, or remorse. He was a cold, hard criminal. I got the feeling that my Siren may have underestimated him. But I continued to keep my body calm and listened. I didn't want to incite him before I knew what I was up against.

"And I always do. I don't give a shit what you do either, if you keep doing fair business with me, Juan. Look, what's all this talk about? First, you have us meet you in this creepy abandoned town in an old warehouse, and then you send my boy out to get the girls while you say we need to talk. Just lay it on me, Juan. What have you heard?" I tried to play dumb like I knew nothing, but there was no way this didn't have to do with my Ol' Lady and what she did for a living. I had been giving Juan's girls new lives for years now, and he hadn't cared before. Something had happened, and the FBI was probably going to need to know this the moment I made it out of that warehouse. If I made it out, that is.

"See? This is why I like you, Reed. You're straightforward. It's why I wanted to talk to you instead of making my assumptions. It's why I wanted to give you a chance to explain and handle things your way before I angered Rafael with this disturbing news." Well, at least I knew we didn't have the whole cartel on our ass, not yet anyway. But I didn't like his tone, even though he was seemingly friendly. "That woman of yours, the one that is the president for the Vipers, there was something not right about her. I just knew it in the way she acted. At first, I just thought she was new to the game. She had obviously just inherited that renegade group from her ruthless father and wasn't doing a great job filling his shoes. It happens. But when I dug deeper, I found out that my original instinct was right. And because we are friends, I thought you should know because if we go down, you will go down with us."

Shit! He was about to blow Elena's cover. I just knew it, and I had to think quick, especially as he was giving me the chance to play dumb like I had no idea about her. But I couldn't let this make it back to Rafael. I knew that. Anything was better than letting this cartel know Elena was with the FBI. She would be as good as dead to the cartel and to the government. I wasn't naïve about how that shit worked. Once you fucked up, there was no more protection for you.

"Why would either of us go down, Juan? Look, this chick is hot and great in bed, that's all I know. I guess I should be more careful who I take home with me. But, really, how bad can she be?" I played it up, making sure he thought I didn't care for her and had no intimate knowledge beyond what her pussy felt like. I was hoping the sleazeball would buy it. I had made a good sleazeball myself when I first became Prez. Surely, I had been convincing.

"That woman is not who you think she is, Reed. She is an undercover agent for the FBI. She means to turn us all in for sex trafficking and who knows what else. My hope is that I told you in enough time for you to dispose of her before she gets too much information. I don't want any trouble for having dealings with the wrong people, and I know you don't ever want to meet Rafael." There was a threat in there somewhere, but I could tell this Rafael person wouldn't be happy with Juan if he had to come after two MCs that Juan made deals with to save his ass. There was a chance for me to get out of this unscathed and get to Elena before it was too late.

"You're fucking kidding me?" I acted angry, forcing myself to turn red with rage. "That fucking cunt!"

"I know this must come as a shock, but she was chosen by the FBI for a reason." I nodded, acting like I was cooling down and becoming grateful for his information. I pulled out my wad of cash for him and went to shake his hand.

"Thank you, Juan, for giving them the chance to deal with this before it's too late. I have an entire MC full of people she could put in danger, all because I was thinking with my dick." Juan held out his hand to shake, looking satisfied with my response, and that's when I turned on him. It was the fastest I had ever pulled out a gun in my whole life. I shot him down in cold blood like it was the fucking wild west and ran for my life to the van, glad as hell that all the women were already in there.

"Fucking drive, Seamus!" I screamed. He looked at me with fear in his eyes. He had heard the gun shot. He took off like a bat out of hell as we saw Juan's associate running into the warehouse to see what has happened. I got him within range and shot him. I didn't look back to see if he was dead or only injured. We had to get the fuck out of there.

"Don't ask any questions," I told Seamus. "get to the next town, and we'll split up. You get these girls home and you out that bar on lockdown. The whole club needs their pieces on them always. Protect the women. All of them." Seamus nodded. I knew I could count on him in this time of need. He was a great friend.

I picked up my cell and dialed a number I had saved only for such emergencies as this. I called Kristie, Elena's handler.

"I just fucking killed Juan, Kristie. I shot his associate and took the girls. He knew who Elena was. He's more cunning than we thought. It sounded like he hasn't told anyone yet, but because I shot him, they'll be after us soon. They'll kill us." I was in a panic. "I've got to come for Elena. In the meantime, get your shit together and figure out what the hell we're going to do."

She answered in as calm a voice as she could have, and I could hear Elena in the background with John. Thank goodness, she was with them and safe right now. "Alright, we'll do all we can to keep her safe. We'll see you soon."

CHAPTER 17

Reed

Every time I crossed the border of the next state or stopped to fill my tank, I found myself looking over my shoulder. It was only a matter of time before the fucking cartel got wind of Juan's death, and they were not going to let it go unpunished. Even if I had succeeded in taking out the associate and only witness on Juan's side, they would surely figure out who he had made his latest deal with.

There was nothing that got past the leader of a cartel like that. They were all-seeing and all-knowing like a God, which was why I hated that the FBI had gone from getting Elena involved with a hard ass MC to making her give up sensitive information about a cartel. This cartel had a reach that was fucking miles long. They dealt with more than just women, and I knew that. Juan was only a small piece in a larger operation, and I was scared shitless right now.

I had just won a woman that could stand by my side as an equal, and be in my bed each night without fail. I wasn't ready to lose her yet. And I sure as hell wasn't going to let her lose me. She has gone through enough in her life. I was here to make sure it was better from here on out.

I was finally approaching Cincinnati, driving so fast other motorists probably thought the devil himself was on my back. That's what it felt like as I navigated through the heavy morning traffic of the city. The highway was backed up to the point that I had little choice but to fly through the shoulder and passed all the traffic to make sure I got to her.

I had left Elena to her own devices long enough, and I wasn't about to make her wait any longer to get to safety. I had a slight idea of what the bureau was going to have is to do. They would be giving us new identities of some kind and putting us into hiding.

It would mean that our MCs would have to be run by the VPs for the time being. I didn't know how I felt or how my club would feel about that. I had never had to do that for more than a day before.

I knew that Dmitri would take care of things for Elena. He had been doing it most of the time anyway, even keeping the Vipers sane under Jimmy's iron fist all these damn years. I could only hope my boy, Max, would pull through for me and keep my friends and family safe. I had to worry about Elena and me right now.

I sped up to the building where we met Kristie and John in the past. I wasn't sure if Elena was there or if she was at her house or staying somewhere else entirely. I felt a bit out of the loop.

So, I calmed myself and picked up my phone, turning it on for the first time since I had hopped on my bike an hour out of Laredo. I had kept it off because I didn't want anyone, government, cartel, or otherwise to be able to use the thing to track where I was going. Every decision I had made from the moment I shot Juan was to give us enough time to get out of there safely.

I dialed Kristie's number, unsure if Elena's phone would have been changed out by now. If anyone else in the cartel had found her out, who knew what other information they had on her. It was a good thing Kristie had convinced her to come to Cincinnati to meet to discuss the cartel instead of talking over the phone about it

---

"Reed, is that you?" It was Elena's voice, and I had never been so relieved to hear it. I was overcome with emotion, but right now wasn't the time for breaking down. I could do that once we got to our destination.

"It's me, Siren. I told Kristie I was coming for you. I'm in Cincinnati, and I need to know where to find you. Are you at your apartment?"

"No," she answered, sounding distressed. I doubt she had been able to sleep since Kristie gave her the news in whatever way she saw fit. For all I knew, Elena hadn't even known for sure if I was alright. "They let me go back there last night to grab a few things and then that was it. I am staying at Kristie's now, and there have been armed agents around us pretty much the whole time. You need to tell me what's going on. They've told me almost nothing." She was more in panic mode than I was, but the answers would have to wait.

"You're going to have to wait for that, babe. We need to get the hell out of here. Text me the address, and I'll come for you. Get the plan from Kristie because we need to fly." I hung up because time was of the essence here. I wasn't' going to hang around and wait for them to find us in her hometown. I took off down the road, glad that the address came through quickly. It wasn't too far, and I found myself at a large downtown high rise in five minutes flat.

I took the elevator up to the tenth floor and found 1021, the unit that Elena had said Kriste lived in. I could see several well-planted people with guns if I looked hard enough, but they weren't pointed in my direction. The FBI probably knew every time I took a piss at this point, so I had nothing left to worry about there.

I knocked on the door, and Kristie was the one that answered, pulling me in quickly and bolting the door behind her. "Fuck, Reed, it took you long enough," she huffed, and I could chortle at that. Off duty, I kinda liked her.

She led me into the depths of the luxury apartment where I found a distraught Elena waiting for me. I took the time to meet her embrace and kiss her reassuringly before we got down to business.

"Now, what the fuck's the plan?" I asked, looking at Kristie and the two black-suited agents that had made themselves at home there for the time being.

"There is an armored vehicle, completely unmarked, waiting outside in the lot for you. You get three bags of luggage altogether, and they are already packed inside the vehicle. One of them will contain your new phones, identities, and anything else you need to change your appearance once you reach your destination.

"Both of you are to lay low and to go into hiding. We will keep your motorcycle safe, Reed, and there will be a car waiting for you where we're taking you. I highly suggest you don't leave once you're there. The two agents that are taking you will also stay with you for protection until the bureau gives the all clear. The only contact you will have is us. I want you to understand; this is no vacation." I nodded, I totally understood that. I looked over at my Ol' Lady's pursed lips and knew she didn't like the talking to.

"So, where are we going?" she asked, standing up and putting her arm in mine. She looked as ready to go as ever.

"You know we aren't going to tell you that. We can't risk you calling someone on the way and putting them and yourself in more danger. The FBI is extending this protection to you because of the contact we have with you and your long-standing successes," Kristie explained, flinching at her own formality. "They won't be so forgiving if you decide to ruin this for yourself."

I got the gist of what she meant. If we stepped out of line, we lost our protection and possibly our lives. Elena would certainly lose her job. I wasn't planning on breaking any rules right now, no matter how bad ass I thought I was.

"Yeah, I get it," Elena grumbled. I could see tears welling up in Kristie's eyes. Elena had told me that Kristie was much more than her handler. They were best friends. I was finally getting a tiny glimpse of that.

Kristie came up and threw her arms around Elena in a tight hug. "Be safe," she whispered to her, and Elena hugged back and nodded. I didn't feel a whole lot of confidence coming from Siren at that moment, and I hoped our long trip in the car would be able to give me a chance to change her mind. If she lost confidence now, then all was lost. There was nothing left there to save.

"It's gonna be okay, Siren," I told her, kissing the side of her head as the two agents led us out of the apartment and down the elevator. It felt a little bit like the walk to death row, but I wasn't going to voice that out loud. I knew that being whisked away by the FBI was no guarantee of anything, but I had to hold out hope that we would find a new and safe life for now and that they would be able to bust the cartel quickly.

"If you say so," she said, as we were led to the parking lot and towards a large, black Infiniti that was waiting for us. The agents showed us that there were two bags packed in the trunk and one sitting in the middle of the back seat. That must have been the one that had our new phones in it.

We reluctantly handed our own phones over and got in the vehicle with lightly tinted windows. A male and female agent were dressed in casual clothes in the front seat, ready to take us to our destination. I couldn't help but wonder where our home was going to be for the next several weeks or months until the cartel was no more.

I reached out and held Elena's had as we took off, squeezing it with love. There were no words right now that would make any of this go away, so I was going to have to wait for the right ones to come to me later.

In my mind, I said my goodbyes to Seamus, Daisy, and all the others back at the club. My family was going to have to get on without me, and I just hoped that my leaving with Elena would mean they could do so in peace.

CHAPTER 18

Elena

I looked around nervously even though I knew that there were two fully armed agents standing only yards away and that Reed and I both had our weapons on us. We stopped at a pay phone not too far from the hotel. We were outside a gas station with only two pumps. We needed to call the MCs and let them know what they needed to do right now. I still wasn't at liberty to reveal that I was with the FBI to anyone, and I knew how close I was to being retired and losing my protection if I broke or even bent one rule. This was not the time to be bad ass, rogue, Elena. I needed to follow the rules, and so far, I had, right down to cutting my hair. I felt strange and kept reaching out to grab only air, but we needed to look different, and that we did.

I had been given what I could only describe as suburban mom clothes; midrise jeans and jean jackets with shirts in bright colors that only showed mild cleavage. That plus the more conservative cut of my fiery hair made me appear to be even older than my actual 27. Although on an average day I was used to still looking like I was in my early 20s despite my scars.

Looking at Reed was hard to stomach right now for me. When he took his clothes off, I was sure he would still turn me on like always. They couldn't take away his ripped chest or the taste of his skin and lips. But they had made him dye his black hair to blonde and completely get rid of any sign of facial hair. He looked quite uncomfortable in his clothes that made him resemble the kind of guy that would take meetings at work by going to a golf course. If we weren't in such a dire situation, I was certain I would laugh.

I waited my turn for the phone patiently, as Reed tried to communicate with the MC without giving too much away. I felt bad for bringing him into this. This wasn't his responsibility, and he was having to act like he was an agent himself and entrust his whole MC to a man who had ever really had control over it before. I knew that my girls would help hold things down at the club and help the women Seamus had brought back to the bar start on a new life. I could just see Daisy taking charge in my mind's eye.

Reed finally hung up, and I could see the strain on his face as he backed up so I could take over with the phone. I looked back at the agents that were our 24/7 babysitters, and they were getting impatient. Their names, as far as we were told, were Sally and Ronald, and they were both in their 40s. They seemed nice enough, but I knew protecting another agent who had probably fucked up was not the most glorious job in the universe for them. They probably thought they were getting this job because they were getting old or out of shape. To think I was around a decade or so from that fate was scary.

I got up to the phone and dialed Dmitri's number, not sure what to expect on the other end. I hadn't got much of a chance to have a conversation with Dmitri and get to the bottom of whether the Vipers were aware of my job with the FBI. Jimmy obviously knew, but how many people had he revealed that information to?

Dmitri answered the phone, sounding suspicious of the random number. "Dmitri," I barked. "It's me, the Prez." I wasn't about to say my name over the phone right now to anyone anymore. I had no idea how Juan had ended up figuring that I was an undercover agent with the FBI, but there were no more chances I could afford to take. "Something bad has happened with the cartel, and things have gone south. I have to go off the grid for a while, and I need to know you're going to take care of things there. If you need any help, the Skulls Renegades will happily be of service. But don't expect to purchase any more girls from Juan, and definitely, don't contact him."

"Should I be worried, boss?" Dmitri asked with concern. The man had taken a real liking to me once I took over the MC and I wondered if it was because I had made sure all the other families were safe and cared for by not letting the club go to shit. But maybe it was more than that.

"I need you to worry about the MC right now. Make sure there's muscle around and just keep things running. I'm going to worry about me. Don't you do that for me." I hung up before I got emotional about it. I had heard about agents being put into hiding before, but I had never thought, even with all my recklessness, that I was going to be one of those agents someday.

I took Reed's hand and went back over to the car and got in, anxious to get back into the house and be alone with Reed; as alone as we were going to be sharing the place with the two agents. But that was our life now. We had new names, new jobs, and a new place to live. The only thing to tell me about where I now were the welcome signs to the city; Everett, Washington.

The bureau had rented a house in a nice and quiet neighborhood just minutes from the coast, but despite the beauty of the blue waters, it seemed too cold to bother going to the beach. Everyone we saw headed there wore wetsuits.

As soon as we got into the house, I headed straight for the bedroom I was sharing with Reed. I shut the door the minute he was in there with me and turned on the television for nothing more than distracting noise. Laying down on the bed, I crossed my arms over my chest.

"Babe, you need to quit beating yourself up over this. This was bound to happen either way. Those cartel assholes, they aren't dummies. We are just lucky that we're both here together and alright. I didn't think anyone is going to find us here." Reed was trying to make me feel better like he had for the last several hours. He was relentless, and it was sweet, but it just wasn't helping.

"I don't think you get it, Reed, what I'm feeling right now," I admitted, sitting up and pulling my knees to my chest. Reed rubbed my back comfortingly.

"Then, why don't you tell me? You don't have to be so damn tough all the time, Siren. I know you aren't weak. You run an MC. You shot the man that killed your mother. You are an FBI agent. I am never going to think you're weak."

He voiced what my fear was deep down. I was a tough girl; I had to be. I grew up to be an even tougher woman. If I had learned anything from my relationship with Dick, it was a lesson about not being too vulnerable and too soft. But maybe with Reed, I could find that happy medium.

"Reed, I've always been this amazing FBI agent. I always went rogue and made up the rules. I pissed off my superiors more times than I can count. But what all those times had in common was that I never failed. I got the job done, and I got it done better than any other agent I knew of. They loved me, and I felt so strong and powerful. When I got serious with my ex, Richard, you know the one that you met in Cincinnati?" Reed nodded. We had gotten deep into each other's pasts since being together, but I hadn't really gotten into details about Richard other than that we were engaged, and he cheated. It didn't really seem necessary to talk about until now. "Well, he was concerned about me being in the field. You know it's a dangerous job. You've seen it firsthand. So, he asked me if there was something else I could do while still being involved in the FBI. I asked to be trained as a handler. I would get to be at home and be protected, giving the orders to somebody else who would be in danger. I did it because I thought Richard was being sweet and looking for the woman he loved."

"It's not right to ask those things of someone you love; asking them to change something about them. I can tell you love what you do. Even if it worries me, I could never ask you to quit just for me." I smiled and leaned over into his arms.

"I appreciate that," I told him. "But it wasn't even just the job. I just didn't know it until I saw him with his secretary balancing on his balls. He had slowly changed everything about me; the clothes I wore, the places I went for fun…He softened me to the core, prepping me to be his perfect little trophy wife, and then he still didn't want me. As soon as we were over, I went running to Kristie and begging her for a job in the field. I wanted to prove to myself that I was still the woman

I had been before I met Richard, but that's not how this is turning out. I'm afraid this is just proof I can't do this anymore."

"Babe, you can do anything you set your mind to, I know that. You have now saved eight women from the life of sex trafficking. You have brought two MCs together to do legitimate work. There's nothing to scoff at there." I hadn't thought about it that way, and I realized that I might have found a new calling for myself without trying to. I loved the exhilarating danger in the field, but being the Prez of an MC and Reed's Ol' Lady felt like an amazing place to be. It felt like home.

I looked in Reed's eyes with a lot of thankfulness. Thankfulness he had risked his life to take out Juan and come for me. I pulled his face to mine and kissed him passionately, pulling him down on top of me in the bed. His hand snaked up my shirt to massage at my right breast, causing me to moan into his mouth. Being with Reed was the perfect distraction from our current predicament, and I wanted to take full advantage of that.

I pressed myself up against him, wriggling my hips against his pants. I could feel that he was already hard inside of his ridiculous khakis. So, I reached down and took them off as fast as I could, letting those and his boxers slide to the edge of the bed.

Reed balanced himself over my body as I slid my own pants down, revealing my wet and wanting pussy. His face dived in, lapping at my sweetness as I arched my back into the pleasure of his motions. I reached down to let my fingers run through his hair, which was now bleached like a California Ken doll. It was soft, though, and familiar, as I used it to hold his face to my aching center, just wanting more. Being in bed with Reed was the best comfort a woman could ask for.

His tongue slid in and out of my wet pussy like a pleasant snake, and I moaned softly at the sensation. But even as I felt my body getting warm, letting me know I was close, I knew it wasn't going to be enough. I wanted to feel him too.

I whimpered, feeling deprived of his body. Then, he licked up to my navel, and I sighed as he spread my legs wide, letting his thick cock make its way inside of me. I had missed this. I needed this.

I slid my nails up his back, scratching and letting out all my emotions that way, probably leaving long marks along his skin. He bent down to nip at my neck in response to my own violence. My whole body tensed up, loving this new edge to our love making. It was raw and desperate and sad and angry. It was amazing.

I moaned and bucked my hips within his set rhythm until I screamed his name, not caring if the other agents could hear me

CHAPTER 19

Daisy

I had a feeling that the reason that Reed and Elena were not around and not in contact was because something awful had happened. Seamus had come back with the girls in utter shock, telling us he had heard gunshots and then Reed came out looking like he'd seen a ghost. They'd split up somewhere in Texas with Seamus having orders to bring the girls home and let Reed go. That was all he knew and all we were left with nothing other than the orders to keep each other safe and trust no one. I knew the cartel we had been doing dealings with was nasty, and I could only imagine what they might do to anyone of us, especially Reed if he had harmed or killed one of them. I was nervous as hell, and tension was already high because Kyle had been around more and more since Reed had disappeared.

I had to admit, though, as annoying as hell as he was and as many awful memories as he brought back to me, he was doing a decent job at keeping morale up. He was even helping with getting the women Seamus had got back nice and settled. It really confused me, because I had my eyes set on someone else already. I wanted to keep to myself for a little while longer, but it was hard even to know that was right with my epic ex running around the bar all day long like the ghost from Christmas fucking past.

It was around eight or nine at night, and almost everyone was in the bar, having a drink and shooting the shit like they always did. It seemed like the most normal night we had in a little bit. But that soon changed when a group of Mexican men stormed into the place with guns of all sizes, shooting it up like it was war.

I screamed with the rest of the girls and dropped behind the bar, trying to pull as many people back there with me as I could. The shots just didn't stop, and I knew some of our men had pulled out their guns and joined in the crossfire. Deep down, I was afraid that would only make it worse. How many people got killed from crossfire in MC fights? There were a lot I knew in my time on this Earth, and I didn't want to see it happen to anyone I loved. But as I crouched behind the bar and prayed that the guns would run out ammo and the men would leave without taking prisoners, I knew that there couldn't be that much gunfire without a loss of life or limb.

I began to flat out cry, hugging Michelle to me. She was the only comfort I had. I was scared shitless that I was going to be taken once again, become one of those women sold into sex slavery down south. It wasn't a life I would live through after what had happened to me in the past. I would fuckin' slit my wrists before I did it again.

Eventually, the guns quieted inside, and I could hear the men pushing the Mexicans outside, out into the open. I would go to jail any damn day if the noise and chaos was just seen and heard by somebody who could come and make it stop.

Jenna crawled over to me and pointed to the basement entrance. Just in case they came back in, that was probably the best bet. So, we began to lead all the women, crawling until we got to the stairs, and we ran as fast as we could, locking ourselves inside until someone could come tell us it was safe to get out.

I knew if a god existed I wasn't on such good terms with him, but I bowed my head and prayed anyway. I found I wasn't the only one. What was going to be left of the bar and the people I called my family after this was all over?

We held hands together down there for hours until we were too exhausted to keep ourselves awake.

***

I climbed into the ambulance like the fuckin' softie that I was, looking down at the man I once loved, fighting for his life. He looked like hell, with blood all over him. My heart was torn. Even as I hated this man's guts for abandoning me, I couldn't let him die alone. I held his hand and cried for the second time in the last 24 hours, not knowing if the EMTs had even been able to get to any of our injured members on time. I didn't even want to think about the dead ones we lost back at home. If I could just get through this one, I could worry about the rest later.

My damn cell began to ring in my pocket, and I picked it up. I had never been so fuckin' received to hear the Prez's voice. "Oh, my god, Reed!" I screamed, losing my shit right then and there. "They fuckin slaughtered us. They blew bullet holes through the place for hours. Where the hell are you?"

"The most I can tell you is that Elena and I left to keep something like this from happening. I couldn't be more fucking sorry we were wrong. Dais', Dais', just tell me. Tell me who we lost. How bad is it?"

I could hear the distress in his voice. Someone had gotten to him first and told him what happened. Nothing was more humiliating or devastating for a Prez than having your members gunned down in an attack like that. I wondered how Elena was feeling and if the Vipers had met a similar fate.

I meant to tell him about the four we lost, including one of the girls he had saved, but there was only one person on my mind right now to speak of. "Kyle, your fuckin' brother. He thought he was a bad ass and pushed them outside and off the property. He's got bullet holes all in him and there was so much blood. It doesn't look good, Reed. I'm in the ambulance with him now, and they're working on him as best they can. But he just looks so red and so out of it, Reed. Please, tell me you're coming back. We don't know what to do without you."

It was selfish to ask because I knew the two of them were probably safer where they were. But the MC would fall apart now without his leadership. And obviously being in hiding had done nothing.

"I think we're both coming back. We're going to figure this out, Dais'. Just hang in there. Do you want to talk to Elena?" He knew what the answer was before I even said it, and the phone was passed off to her. I could hear her tears before she even said a word.

"Shit, Daisy. I'm so fucking sorry for leaving you guys behind. I was just so sure you'd be safe if we disappeared. How can I ever make this up to you?" She sounded just as distraught as I was. In just a brief time she had made herself fit in with us like family. She was like the sister I never had. I just wanted to hug her so we could both know it would be okay, but I couldn't.

"It's not your fault, Elena. I know it ain't. They were sick men; assholes. This was bound to happen one day. I just hope we find a way to make them pay for what they did." It was the truth. I was seein' red.

"You're damn straight we will." I knew when Elena said something like that, she meant it.

CHAPTER 20

Elena

It was under cover of night that we returned to what was left of the bar. It had been blown through with bullet holes, at least in the actual front half of the building. A couple of the rooms had caught some damage as well; including Reed's office. Tears had poured from me until my eyes had run dry. I was sure I wouldn't be able to produce any again for a long time.

As I slid into bed with Reed, it was hard to think of it as a safe place anymore, even though I was glad to be home. I couldn't help but feel a deep regret for letting the FBI hide us away instead of staying and fighting with our MCs.

Reed turned over and looked at me, and I could see the same tired guilt in his eyes. I stroked my fingers through his still light-colored hair. It had grown on me a little since we'd been gone, but I was happy to see his five-o'clock shadow again. I leaned in and kissed him, tears running down my face, believing my previous thought. I pressed myself up against him, only his boxers and my cami and matching panties to keep our bodies apart. His warmth was comforting and real; the only solid and tangible thing I had to go on right then.

We easily slipped into each other, my panties down to my toes and then tangling in the blankets before he unfurled his cock. He slid his warm member into me, making love to me slowly and surely, the way I needed it right now. There was sadness in our rocking motions that we shared as a held on for dear life. Soon, I was shivering in his arms as his warmth spilled inside of me. It was the only way I was going to sleep that night.

***

I hung up the phone and sat down at the bar, or what was left of it, feeling drained. It had taken all the convincing within me to get the FBI to let me go back Tennessee before they had caught Rafael Ramirez as we knew his full name to be now. Luckily, they had already apprehended a few of his associates on their way back into Mexico and were able to bust one location where they were holding a good fifteen girls hostage in terrible conditions. My career was about to burst open, but all I could think about was all the losses that had taken place because we had underestimated Juan and the cartel. The repairs were slow coming, and we had held a memorial for those lost already. But the one piece of good news we had was that Kyle was coming home from the hospital any minute now.

Daisy had headed to the hospital to pick him up. He had died on the table during surgery several times, but he had somehow pulled through. I had never seen Daisy so upset or confused before. The minute I'd come back, she ran into my arms and spilled the beans about all her conflicted feelings. There was another man she had been with for a bit, but it wasn't too serious yet. She didn't tell me who, and I didn't push her. She had also told me that when she saw Kyle laying there and dying, all the feelings, she had once felt for him came rushing right back into her heart like they had never left. I felt for her. I couldn't imagine the emotional rollercoaster she had been on ever since he came back, and now with a near death experience added in, it was just impossible to fathom.

The two walked in the door, Kyle with an obvious limp and looking worse for the wear. He wasn't going to be 100 percent for quite a while, but as I understood it, a lot of the members owed him their life. He led the fight back against the cartel and put them on the run.

Everyone in the bar cheered for his arrival, and I tried to put a smile on my face for the sake of what was appropriate and what Dais needed from me, but I just wasn't feeling it.

Reed turned around and grabbed a beer from behind the bar and raised it, tapping it with his keys to get everyone's attention. I was sure he was going to give a toast in thanks to his brother, but instead, he turned to me.

Everyone watched as Reed grabbed my hand and looked right into my eyes. I had no idea what was going on. "Babe, you have been my everything through thick and thin since you got here. I would trust you with my life. I once told you that you were my ride or die when I gave you this cut." He reached over and felt the leather of my jacket between his fingers. I looked at him curiously, but he gave away nothing.

"I kept thinking of ways I could let you know what you meant to me and how to top myself, but it just wasn't coming to me. But then I realized, there was only one fuckin' thing left to do." He got down on one knee, and a collective gasp went around the room. I could feel my hand shaking in his, finally realizing what he was about to do. What the hell was he thinking?

"Life is too damn short, babe, and I want you with me every crazy ass minute of it. So, I want to know, if you'll marry me, and make me the luckiest fuckin' man in the world." I was surprised when I felt the hint of a tear dripping down my cheek. Was this what I wanted, to marry Reed? It hadn't been too long since I was engaged and suffocated and then betrayed. But that didn't matter anymore. Reed knew me inside and out and still loved me. I didn't see the point in turning him down.

I opened my mouth to give him my answer as everyone was watching and waiting.

COMING SOON

REDEMPTION
(SKULLS RENEGADE #2)

Daisy Brown is a tough as nails member of Skulls Renegade MC, and she prides herself on pushing past her demons. But she just watched one of her best friends get proposed to, and she can't help but feel something softening inside of her. She has had a rough time of it, coming out of the worst break up possible with Kyle, the old Prez of Skulls Renegade MC, who left her high and dry when she had to pay the price for his screw up with a loan shark. Now, he's back, and he has gotten injured saving the MC from an attack by a Mexican cartel, and it's hard not to see him as someone she cares for again. The problem is, she's been sneaking around with another prominent member of the MC completely undetected and was almost ready to spill the beans. Daisy finds herself locked in the strangest love triangle she can imagine, needing Kyle's presence to heal from what she has done but wanting to keep the other man in her life tearing up her bedroom late at night.

Coming Soon

Tough as Steele

I'm Brooklyn Harper, a 24-year-old blonde, ambitious model who's determined to find the big break that will get my beauty brand off the ground. I decided that some late-night drinking would help calm my nerves before the big interview with my potential investor. But...after waking up late, alone and naked in a stranger's bed, how am I supposed to sell my brand to the guy whose name I'd been screaming only hours prior?

COMING SOON

CORRUPTED LOVE

As the new face of a modeling agency, Greer Matthews traded the congested LA freeway for the jet-setting lifestyle of the rich and elite.

As she gets closer to the company's stakeholders, she realizes that this lifestyle comes with certain expectations. Ones that take her into a dark shadowy world filled with corruption, greed, and questions about Greer's past.

Assigned a protector, she realizes she is falling in love as the stakes get higher in a game of cat and mouse.

Aleks, the smoking hot legal advisor, is a dream come true for Greer, but Aleks holds secrets regarding her birth parents. Could the dangerous nature of Alek's true identity mark the end of their relationship before it even begins?

Coming Soon

Promised

Mariana

My life changed eight years ago when my captor slaughtered my family in front of my eyes and took me as his own personal trophy.

I thought they would find me – that the clans would look for the last remaining Vasile. They didn't. Instead, they abandoned me like I was nothing.

After being here for years, I'd learned to accept my fate – to accept the hell I was living. Until one day it all went to shit, my daughter was ripped from my arms, I was shot, and the man who saved me

was the one I was promised to all those years ago –
Ion Petran.

But saving me was not enough now that my
parents are gone. He will have to win me over if he
still wishes to be the king of the Vasile clan.

Ion

She's the key to all my success, promised to me
when I was a child.

She's been missing for years, and when I find
her, I'll have everything I've ever wanted.

I found her. Eight years of searching and I found
the woman who would change my life.

I expected a lot of things from her, stupidly of
me, I didn't expect to get more than I bargained for.

The day she turned twenty-one she was supposed to be in my home – her captor stole that from us. He stole her from me, and he'll pay.

No one crosses me, ever.

Made in the USA
San Bernardino, CA
07 November 2017